MW01132591

The Lightning Within Us

By Mary Emerick

Hidden Shelf Publishing House
P.O. Box 4168, McCall, ID 83638
www.hiddenshelfpublishinghouse.com

Copyright @ 2024, Mary Emerick
Hidden Shelf Publishing House
All rights reserved

Artist: Megan Whitfield

Editor: Robert D. Gaines

Graphic design: Rachel Wickstrom

Interior layout: Kerstin Stokes

Publisher's Cataloging-in-Publication data
Names: Emerick, Mary, author.
Title: The lightning within us / Mary Emerick.
Description: McCall, ID: Hidden Shelf Publishing House, 2024.
Identifiers: ISBN 978-1-955893-36-7 (paperback) | 978-1-955893-37-4
(epub) | 978-1-955893-38-1 (Kindle)
Subjects: LCSH Twins--Fiction. | Idaho--Fiction. | Oregon--Fiction. |
Wildfires--Fiction. | FICTION / Disaster | FICTION / Family Life /
General | FICTION / Small Town & Rural | FICTION / Thrillers /
Suspense | FICTION / Nature & the Environment
Classification: LCC PS3605 .M47 L54 2024 | DDC 813.6--dc23

Dedication

Dedicated to the men and women who taught me how to build trails in the mountains of Idaho.

One

She had been dreading September for months. Back in December, it had seemed so far away; she was safe then. The winter had been so long, day after day hard frosts in the valley, cold stars burning holes in the endless night sky, deep snow on the canyon rim, easy to believe that September would never come.

It had been fifteen years since two girls went up a mountain, and only one came down. As she always did on the anniversary, Lina counted what the wilderness took from her the summer she was fifteen. Her father captured by the mountains; her mother betrayed by the sun. The forest took Cassie and never gave her back. Those were the most important of her losses. If she were a tree, she would take pain and become stronger, wrap her new and thicker bark around the scars of the fire or the tracks of the beetle. Instead, she had turned into a woman who hid in shadows.

On the surface, this day on Starvation Road was no different than the day before. Already the winds had shifted up canyon, the heat an almost visible blanket dropping down from the sky. There could be fires from the lightning last night, slowly chewing through the dry grass, climbing up the Trees of Heaven, but for now the sky was clear of smoke.

Lina drove down valley, swerving to avoid the tumbleweeds and trashcans littering the road, debris of last night's wind. The locals call it windsomnia, that combination of wind and lack of sleep that keeps someone awake through the night, revisiting their regrets, cursing their troubles. It was a rare one who could block out the sound of wind slamming into windows, lifting shingles off roofs. In the mornings, everyone ventured out of their houses, gathering back what the wind had borrowed.

Nobody lived up here on the Oregon side of Hells Canyon because they wanted to be known. Not Lina, not Joe, not Lucy ...

Joe Grider hadn't come last night or the night before. If he had left for good, everything Lina had carefully punched down would erupt to the surface. She had worked too hard to have that happen. Maybe he would be at Lucy's house.

From the tiny outpost of Imnaha, Lina would need to navigate twelve more grueling miles. The tires of her ancient Bronco bounced over the shot rock that served as the road; a dead-end, one-lane dirt drive that grew greasy with rain, impassible in a downpour.

Twisted hackberry trees, white-flowering mock orange and head-high poison ivy crowded the road as though the brush was trying to erase the sun. On a clear day this created a dizzying mix of shadow and light that could send a driver off the cliff with vertigo. In the end, nothing was a match for the sun. It beat down without mercy.

In the summer, when the temperatures scraped one hundred degrees, rattlesnakes unfurled like flags across the simmering road. Starvation Road reminded Lina of a rattlesnake, curving deep into a scorched yellow mountain. It looked dangerous enough to prevent all but the desperate.

It was easy to stay hidden on Starvation Road. Like everyone's secrets, the houses Lina passed were concealed behind years of overgrown feral blackberry thickets and self-imposed isolation. Gates were locked tight with large padlocks and weeds were allowed to grow head-high to obscure entrances to dirt driveways.

Lina recalled a neighbor she had seen out walking, a slight, harmless man in overalls. She and others had waved to him countless times, his history unknown to anyone until the FBI arrived.

Starvation Road was that kind of place. The sun went down early and there were hours of darkness before it decided to come back. You recognized your neighbor from down the road, but you didn't ask too many questions. It was a place where Lina figured nobody would track her down. Where she could forget that one night. It wasn't working out that way.

"The whole world forgets about you once you turn off the county road," Joe Grider liked to say.

Lina had banked everything on that being true.

❖ ❖ ❖

On the wash-boarded main road that slung itself along the flank of the Imnaha River, she pulled over at Lucy's place, a white farmhouse dating from the 1940s. Joe's board cabin was out back. No Chevy there, but Lucy was in her garden doing chores. She didn't look eighty years old, despite her frosty hair. Lina was tempted to floor it, seeing that Joe wasn't around, but Lucy had seen her. She rolled down the passenger window, calling over the sound of the river.

"Seen him?"

Lucy, her arms full of zucchini, shook her head. "Not here,

honey. Left a couple of days ago. His rig was full of camping gear, like he was going to be gone a good long time."

"Did he say where he was going?"

"No, sure didn't, honey. Maybe down the crick a ways?" Lucy pointed at the creek. "I'd imagine you'll be seeing him again before long. But who knows with Joe. He's not an easy keeper."

She dumped the vegetables into a basket and approached the car. "He paid his rent up for the month, left an envelope at my front door. So, I imagine he'll be back. But, honey, you know I've tried to tell you. We all have. The man's a charmer, but his stories don't add up. He's told so many lies his mouth has forgotten what the truth tastes like."

She was right. Joe Grider was not the kind of man a woman left. He left them. He was famous for it, even though he had only been here three years tops. The women in the canyon had told Lina. They ticked off each one on their fingers: the hippie girl who worked in the bakery two years ago, one of the Starthistle women, was it Amelia? The pilot lady who had the flight service contract for a while, her too. Up and left them all, the gossipers said with a satisfied sigh. What was unspoken was this: you're next, get ready. They were not being mean, not really. They were just invested in their vision of Joe. In their lonely minds, he was the man they had let get away fifty years before, the one they still dreamed about while their husbands snored next to them. While a man like Joe was around, there was still room to believe that their real lovers might return, full of regrets and promises. Sweeping them off their feet, telling them that things would be different, this time.

"I know it," Lina said to Lucy. She knew better than to say more, but the words tumbled out before she could stop them. "Last April, he took me into the canyon. He's never taken any woman with him before. That's got to mean something."

Lucy's watery blue eyes took in the rims far above them. "Did he take you to the old Cochrane place? Show you the trees of heaven?"

"How did you know?" Lina could not hide a feeling of unease. Was Lucy watching her? What did she know?

Last April, she and Joe had dropped into Hells Canyon on a forgotten trail, hiking down from spring into summer. There hadn't been much left of the settlers who had once lived on the bench far below the rim, just pieces of an old plow. Trees were clustered in a long line from a corral as far down the creek as she could see. They were a deep shade of green among the subdued brown of the canyon, their branches feathering out in long arcs. They looked alien, like they belonged on another planet. As she looked up at them, though, there was something familiar, as if she had seen them before.

"What are they? They don't even look real."

"Smell the air," Joe had said. "Smells like a gang of skunks, right? That's those trees. That's how you recognize them, that odor. They're called Trees of Heaven. Great name, eh? Too bad they're more like trees of hell."

He saw her puzzled expression.

"Turns out, these trees are killers," he continued. "They make a chemical that destroys other plants near them. Gives them more room to grow, less competition for water and sun. Pretty soon, these trees take over the whole piece of ground."

"But why are they here?"

"Settlers brought them in for shade ... *and* they grow fast. Fifty feet in twenty-five years, they say. Shade was a necessity, living down here. Feel that sun? Imagine it in August, a thousand times hotter than this. Chinese laborers brought them too, for medicine. The bark is supposed to cure all sorts of ailments. Even baldness." He laughed.

"Didn't they know the trees would kill?" she asked.

"Maybe they did and maybe they didn't. I'm not going to judge the folks who lived here. Sometimes you need to make a choice. You just do the best you can with it. But maybe they made a deal with the devil."

Joe tilted his head back for a long swallow of water. Wiping his mouth, he said, "You just plain can't make it without shade down here. Or maybe they didn't know and found out later. Maybe they tried to get rid of the trees, but it didn't take. Trees like this love fire, so you can't burn them out. The only way to kill them is to cut them and spray them with serious herbicide. They try to live as fiercely as they can. As do we all."

In the canyon, Lina had stared up into the tops of the trees, shading her face with her hand. It seemed to her that the story of the Trees of Heaven was like any other decision that came with unexpected consequences. The settlers were now blessed with shade, but the trees had expanded up and down the draws, killing off the native plants that once grew there. Once again, she was reminded of the finality that came with a choice.

"Joe, how do you know all this?" Lina already knew the answer.

In just three years, Joe had wormed his way into the canyon peoples' lives. They lent him tools, tossed back shots with him in the tavern, and winched his truck out of the ditch in a snowstorm. Lina watched this relaxed familiarity with longing and curiosity. How did Joe walk right up to strangers, swapping stories and jokes with such confidence? It was never that easy for her.

Joe headed to the café in the early morning, sat there with his cup of coffee, plain black, and listened. He hung over fences talking to ranchers. He warmed a bar stool in the tavern, mouth shut and ears open. It was simple, he said. People wanted to tell their stories.

"You're a puzzle, Taz," Joe had said more than once. She knew that she kept an invisible barrier between them, only giving him the barest of details. She always stopped herself before saying more, but she could sometimes imagine telling him everything, not quitting until it was too late. He would leave for good if he knew it all.

❖ ❖ ❖

"Joe talks about Hells Canyon all the time," Lucy said. "Like it's an adventure to go there. To us, to my people, it's part of our history. My parents knew the people who lived down on the river and up on the benches. I knew them too. They were real. All of them burned out, starved out, gave up, or found something better. Government paid for or stole some land, depending on who you talk to. And don't forget the Niimiipuu," she said, using the real name of the Nez Perce. "They were there before us. That's a whole 'nother story there. It's not a playground to any of us."

But there they were, the two of them last spring like tourists, blundering around the old foundations, laying out sleeping bags in the remnants of the corral. It had been thoughtless, Lina realized now, for them to view the abandoned places as curiosities for them to explore when people had fought and lost everything trying to keep that land. She was overcome with how little she knew about this place ... and how she would never fit in.

"Joe said something about moving on, though," Lucy said.

She seemed ready to settle in for a good long talk. Lina pressed her foot lightly on the pedal, ready to get moving. Talking to anyone too long led to making mistakes. But Lucy had insight into Joe, living as close to him as she did. Insight that Lina wished she had.

"But then again," Lucy added, "He always talks about moving on."

Lina nodded. She remembered Joe's skin, as smooth and brown as chocolate milk. The way he talked about leaving. "There's other places, Taz," he would say. "Places warm enough to strip down to your skin, not either freezing or sweating like it is here. Ice cream, we could eat ice cream again in winter. Drop down to sea level, go someplace that's not as steep as a cow's face, see what life is like in a little easier place. You could come with me, you know. Nothing's left to hold you here. Are you in?"

Lina thought, once again, that she knew why people talked about Joe and why they were so drawn to him. Joe had what they all wanted: the ability to be free, to swing into a pickup on a bluebird day just because. To leave the roostertail of your dust hanging in the still air. To only come back if you felt like it, and sometimes not even then. Even if they could, most people weren't brave enough to live like Joe.

"Or we could go even farther south," Joe had said. "There's a mountain range down there in Nevada called the Barrens. The darkest sky in the lower forty-eight. Thousands of stars, so many they overlap each other. The Great Basin, where all the rain that falls stays there. Feels like a guy should get himself to a place like that before he dies. Before all the Californians come in with their second homes. Before it's all ruined."

Lucy leaned into the car window, eyeing Lina closely. "Listen, honey. You came in here ten years ago like a spooked rabbit. Won't come to our potlucks or our houses, and that's fine, some folks like to be left alone. But most people who come here thaw after a while once they see we aren't up in their business. You hiding up there on Starvation, it doesn't feel right. Seems like there's something you need to face up to. I notice things. The way you walk, all hunched over like lightning could come out of the sky. Well, honey, if the lightning is meant to get you, walk tall until it does."

Lina drew in her breath. What did Lucy know? Had she seen the stories out of the Yellow River Valley? *Poker face, Tazlina. Don't give anything away.*

Lucy thrust a zucchini at her and grinned. "Last of the crop, hanging on longer than usual. A strange year, so hot so late. Makes a person wonder what's happening on this planet of ours."

Lucy stepped back from the car. "Going to be a hot one," she continued. "You tell the boys down at the shop to bust out the air conditioning, and don't be so cheap. We all need to breathe."

❖ ❖ ❖

Lina blinked back fatigue. It was dangerous to drive this gravel road, no guardrails separating her from the river. People had made mistakes, returning from the tavern on starless nights, thinking they knew every curve and bend by heart.

Still, she had learned to love driving this road, with its dips and turns, the feral apple trees lining the riverbanks, and the ranchers who lifted one finger off the steering wheel as they passed in the other direction. But today none of those soothed her.

What she couldn't tell Lucy, or anyone, was that Joe was her anchor, far more than she wanted to admit. He kept the fear at bay, the set of worries she sat up at night and cataloged. With him around, it seemed possible that one day she could cross off a worry, one at a time; that the knot living in her stomach could unravel.

Where was he? She hadn't seen him knee-deep in the Imnaha river, wetting a fly, and he hadn't been on his latest job, fixing the roof on the one-room school. Maybe he was downriver, building fence for the Rasmussen Ranch, or helping as a spare range rider. He could be up in the high country, hauling only a tarp and matches, searching for the solace he said he found there, nothing but him and endless sky. She never knew where he went for sure, and he rarely told. He just swung back into town unannounced, creating a ripple among all the inhabitants. He'd drop off cash he owed, charm the old ladies at the bakery, and head up to Lina's place. A one-man tidal wave, Lina often thought.

"Get me a road soda, Taz!" he would holler. Then he would jump out of the cab and drain the beer, throwing his head back. "Great day to be alive," he always said, and she wished there was a way to drink him up the way he did the Hamm's. She had been that way once, she thought, before Yellow River. Maybe if she spent enough time studying Joe, she could learn how to be that way again: face as open as the sky, arms wide, irrepressible smile on her face. That was one of the reasons she opened the door for him every time he knocked.

The last time she saw Joe, though, something was wrong. He shifted from foot to foot as though he were standing on hot ash. "You smell like transmission fluid, Taz," he had said. He called her that, liking the short, chopped off syllable instead of the whole mouthful, Tazlina. She didn't mind. It was hard to mind anything about Joe. He was the only one who knew her real name. Except the newspapers in Yellow River, she suddenly realized. It wouldn't take much for him to find out.

❖ ❖ ❖

Even after she had showered and dropped her shop overalls in the wash, the smell of the shop clung to her, absorbed through her skin. She sometimes thought that oil and brake fluid must run sluggishly through her blood by now, a product of all the cars she had lain underneath, their guts breathed in as she worked a wrench. Even her hands hadn't been spared: permanently black under the nails, an old woman's hands.

"I don't get why you work there," Joe always said. "You know I'm not one for working all day. But Jimmy's? You can do better than that garage."

She had thought about it. There wasn't much that didn't shut down in the canyon when the tourists left, but there had to be somewhere else she could talk to someone other than the want-to-be car mechanics, the distressed, the broke, all wanting her to perform miracles with their vehicles.

But she liked the auto shop. It was unpretentiously filthy, with smudged, greasy fingerprints on every light switch, drawers bursting with bolts and hoses, a tiny bathroom with the orange hand cleaner that stripped every bit of moisture from her skin. Every car was a puzzle she could solve, setting each piece inside the other as she removed it from the chassis, dunking the parts in gasoline, taking stiff brushes to batteries. She was the best at the work, unlike Chad who always ended up with parts left over, or Ben, who fell asleep on the creepers. Customers had started to ask for her, because they knew she would come out to the waiting room and sit with them, almost like a doctor would, giving them the bad news. "I can fix it," she would say, "but it's going to run you a thousand dollars." Unlike the others, she could tell the customers where they were going wrong: a heavy foot on the clutch, a reckless disregard for oil changes. She imagined that she made them feel as though there was hope, if they changed their ways.

There was another thing, one she couldn't tell Joe, but that she suspected he knew. Under a car, lying on a creeper in oil-stained overalls, her hair stuffed under a welder's cap, Lina felt safer than anywhere else. Cars gave her no surprises, the way people or the wilderness did. Customers would come in, brows furrowed, claiming that the car had simply quit running for no reason, despite the care they had given it, the washing and waxing, the checking of fluids. She knew that wasn't true. If you paid attention, a car would give you clues long before it gave out.

Under a car, her tools spread in a semi-circle around her, clean rags nearby, she knew that whatever ailment the car had, she could probably fix it. Some things were just symptoms of a bigger problem needing surgery: leaky head gasket, new alternator. There were times when she had to admit defeat and break the bad news: the car was terminal, unlikely to recover, good only for the metal or the parts. But even then, she had worked through all the possible solutions and come to one final conclusion. There was no grey with vehicle maintenance, only black and white. The only decision the customer had was whether they had the money or desire.

"Cars were meant to break," Jimmy always said cheerfully. "So, we might as well benefit. Now go turn some wrenches and make me proud."

❖ ❖ ❖

It was full-on summer as she pulled into the shop yard. Customers crowded the waiting room, each with their own heartbreak. Cars that barely ran, cars they couldn't really afford, cars they needed to nurse along to get to work.

Her heart sank. Standing by a Ford 250 was her father. Why was he here? She hadn't seen him for so long she had started to think that maybe he had disappeared for good, vanished the way other treasure seekers had, lost or dead in some nameless canyon.

"Didn't find it up in the Wind Rivers," he announced. "Damn, I was so sure. But I met a good bunch of guys up there. They have a theory about Hells Canyon. Figured it was so close I should drop by, see if you might have a spot of cash to tide me over. I'll pay you back when we find the treasure."

"How much do you need this time?" she mumbled. If she gave him enough, he would go away.

The big garage door of the shop was open. On the concrete floor, Jimmy gestured to a Chevy with a broken axle as someone behind him cursed over a frozen belt. "On the clock, Lina!" he hollered, pantomiming for her to wrap it up.

"Don't know, Tazlina," her father said as he rolled a cigarette, his hands shaking a little. He had grown a ponytail since she had last seen him, a tangled knot of blond and grey. His arms were scarred and sinewy, his walk marked with a limp. The mountains had beat him up.

"They get younger and younger," he said, puffing carefully, lighting another match on his boot heel. "They call me 'The Old Man of the Mountains.' They say things like they hope they are half as good climbing hills as I am when they're my age.

They think that's a compliment, as if they can't believe some old geezer can walk in the hills. Christ on a cracker."

"You could stop," she said, watching the bleached-out grass in the pasture next door blow in the wind. Just a few months before that same grass had seemed so hopeful, so green, so unaware that its fate was to dry out and die.

"The hell else would I do? I'm not like everybody else. None of us ever were."

She knew he had always thought he was special. That's why he left the family behind, committed to being an adventurer, the same as when he committed to a climb up a mountain. You could try to sidehill out, downclimb, he had told her, but in the end, your mind inexorably carried you along the easiest way, the way the mountain wanted you to go. Only if you were brave, like he was, could you break the pattern.

Lina took a few steps back, scenes from that summer flashing through her mind: her mother, light skin burning in the sun, eyes blank behind enormous sunglasses; her sister's muffled tears, the space where her father had been.

She blinked the memory away and dug in her pocket for a few grimy bills, handing them to her father. With a nod of thanks, he carefully folded them into his wallet. She anxiously glanced at the shop, needing to get back to work.

"I'm so close, Tazlina," her father said. "I can taste it. I know I'm right about where it is."

Nothing new, she thought, tuning him out.

In the shop, Jimmy threw his hands in the air, flourishing his greasy ballcap in her direction. "Whenever you have time for us," he hollered.

Lina acknowledged Jimmy's flair for the dramatic with a small wave, knowing she was his best mechanic.

"Something about you changes when you start to work on a vehicle," Jimmy had told her on one of the nights when it was just them left to close. "Don't take this the wrong way, but nobody really looks at you twice walking down the street. Quiet as an owl hunting a mouse, it's like you're trying not to be noticed ... or maybe you're just scared of your own shadow." He smiled. "But you are magic with a wrench. Never seen anything like it."

❖ ❖ ❖

Her father looked down toward the store where a group of men clustered by a motley assortment of egg-shaped trailers. They all looked the same: furry-faced, lean, dressed in fatigues and spreading maps over a pickup truck's hood. Treasure hunters. She had seen them her whole life, swinging in to pick him up, eyes ablaze, dropping him off weeks later, dejected but resolute.

"I'm going to find it this time," he said. "I can feel it. We're about to crack the code. You'll see, Tazlina."

From the trailers the other men waved and hollered, their words indistinct. "Time's up," he said. "Got to go. One of the guys found a hot spring on Cherry Creek on one of the old Forest Service maps. We'll go down there and poke around. I mean, if you wanted to hide a treasure, where else but Hells Canyon? Am I right or am I right?"

"I don't know, Dad," Lina said. "Seems like people might have already looked there."

"Nonsense. Nobody goes that deep in the canyon in the summer. Fight the snakes and the ivy? Most people stay by the Snake River on jetboats. Hardly anyone walks in the canyon. You told me that yourself. You know, it was because of you living here that I started thinking about the canyon as a likely place. All of the guys, they're focused on Yellowstone or along the Rio Grande. Hell, if it were there someone would have stumbled across it by now. It's got to be in some hellhole out of the way spot like this."

He waved a hand at the waiting hunters. "Be right there. Keep your pants on!" Then to her, "Listen. I wasn't sure whether to tell you this. We were in Yellow River last week, so I went by the old place. It's still standing. Keep meaning to sell it one of these days, not that it would bring in much cash. Showing its age, but still solid."

The lost house. Her mind tried to rebel but failed. For a moment, she was high above Yellow River in that lost, surreal summer.

Her father was still talking, oblivious.

"Anyway, wrestled with it all the way down the canyon, whether I should let you know or not. What good it would be to bring it up. But I'm not one for keeping secrets. So here it is, I ran into one of the Van Allens. Didn't seem too keen on seeing me. Tried to give me the slip, but I recognized him right off, even though it's been years. Ran him down in the beer aisle to ask him a few questions, like why he was back there after all this time. Felt that there might be something fishy about it. Like they might be opening some kind of investigation, something that might concern you. But no, he said, he was back there to live. God knows why he came back, but there you have it."

Suddenly the air felt too thin to breathe. She put a hand out on sun-warmed metal of his car to steady herself. Could it be true? It could be one of the other Van Allens, she told herself, let out of prison or on the run from somewhere else. "Which

Van Allen? I thought they all left."

"Silas, the youngest one. Wasn't that his name? There were only the two of them there that year, right? Him and that girl. Didn't want to say much, that Silas. Think he's keeping a low profile. Can't say as I blame him, after what happened with Cassie and all."

An electric current, hot as lightning, ran through Lina's spine. Silas was back in the Yellow River Valley. Why was he there? Why hadn't he tried to find her?

Her father had moved on to his favorite topic, himself. "I've been chewing on this, Lina. When I get too old to hike, I'll find some high alpine cirque and wait for a blizzard. You'll find me under a whitebark pine somewhere. Don't worry, I'll leave you some clues."

Lina barely heard him. He had said all this before. Instead, she thought of Cassie. How had she imagined that she could ever escape Cassie? Even now, a decade later, she woke up many nights, throat on fire, running to the sink to drown an endless thirst. Cassie would haunt her forever.

"That is, if there are any whitebark left," he said. "Goddamn it, everything good is going away."

"Blister rust," Lina said. "I heard about that." It seemed there were threats everywhere. Cheatgrass, taking over the canyon slopes, a whole ecosystem wiped out. Winters changing, the lake up in Joseph no longer freezing solid, January thaw so warm that people went out without sweaters.

Her father ground out his cigarette on the tailgate, coughing deep in his lungs. "Chin up, Tazlina. Maybe it's all a test from the Man upstairs. If you believe in that kind of thing. Never did, but now I'm starting to wonder. I know one thing though; I named you what I did for a reason. It's time to live up to your name. Don't avoid the hard things."

Lina drowned any possible chuckle. Her father always avoided the hard things. Winter promises were gone once summer came around. When her mother had gotten ill, he had breezed through the hospital on his way to a mountain, dropping off food she couldn't even eat and flowers that choked the air with sticky perfume.

When Lina had been in the bad place, he had never once visited.

"He's like Indiana Jones," Lina's roommate Shari had said. But Lina had wanted a father, not an adventurer.

"Well." He patted her awkwardly on the shoulder. "Hey, wait. Got something for you. I go up to the old place whenever I go through, put up the storm windows, kick the pack rats out, and I go into the Rod and Gun for a couple. When I came out, this postcard was stuck in my wiper. Someone must have seen me and dropped it off. It's addressed to you, at least it has your initials on it. Probably one of your friends from that last summer. Took a peek at it but couldn't make it out. Might mean something to you."

She took the postcard without looking at it. That summer she was fifteen, he had been gone on another treasure hunt. Where had it been, the Uintas, the San Juans? Whichever one it had been, he had said he wasn't coming back until he found Hunter Malone's treasure. That this time it was do or die. He had said other things, too, when her mother had confronted him. Things about how the family they didn't support his dream.

"Dreams don't pay bills," her mother had bristled. "If you go, don't come back."

"He's caretaking the big summer houses, Silas is," her father said. "Oh, you wouldn't recognize the valley now. Whole crop of mansions up on the hill above town, two, three thousand square feet, underground pools, the works. People that come in from California for maybe one weekend a year." He shook his head. "People like that, they get jumpy about anyone near their front porch. Can you imagine? Like one of us would want to break in and steal something. Anyway, they need someone to watch their places for all the weeks they aren't there. That's what Silas is doing. Got himself a nice little business. That boy really got straightened out. More than I can say for any of the other Van Allens. Still got a bunch of them over in the state pen in Twin Falls, cooling their heels on a life with no parole."

"Did he ask about me?" Lina said impatiently. "Silas, I mean. What did he say?"

"Just that if you had a good life going on, that it must have worked out all right for you. Water, bridge, and all that. His family's all gone now. Kind of like ours. That Bert Van Allen, he just up and vanished after being let out of prison. Silas' dad was down in the sugar beets in Burley, probably will be until he drops. Don't think anyone knew where the mother went, but she never came back. As for us, it's just the two of us now, Tazlina. Well, there's your sister, but I haven't seen her in years. Doesn't approve of my lifestyle, she says. Doesn't want me to be a bad influence on her kids, she says."

When Lina didn't answer, he sighed. "I did my best. Your sister, living in the flatlands ... Florida, for Christ's sake. No good rivers in Florida. No mountains! And your mother, hell of a deal. She went fast, at least. Then there's you, in those overalls, wrenching on cars. None of us turned out the way we were supposed to, did we?"

Lina knew what he saw, looking at her. She didn't spend

much time with mirrors, but she knew that she must look older than the backside of thirty. Worry lines had created a map on her face. Thinner than she should be, as if her body held only bones, not water. She was not the girl Silas had known. Would he even recognize her? Once, Lina thought, she and her sister had been beautiful. And they had had no idea.

"Are you sorry that you let them put me in that place?" Lina immediately wanted to erase the question, seeing how his forehead furrowed in response. She had broken the code: speak only of superficial things ... cars, the weather, the treasure.

Plus, she knew her father didn't believe in regret. You made a decision and stuck with it. You released it to the universe, he would say, before whistling down the road.

"No use in revisiting the past," he said now, slapping his hat on his jeans to release dust from some other place. His face shut tight against her. She should have known better.

"When will you be back through?" An easier question.

He shrugged. "Can't say. Depends on what we find down in Cherry Creek. Should be able to tell as soon as we get there. Tomorrow, maybe? If we don't find anything there, we've got ideas about someplace up in the Pasayten. Maybe the Bob after that, up near McCall. Still plenty of summer left for searching."

"Hey, Dane!" a burly woman called. She wore an overflowing tube top and a sarong tied around her waist. Her feet were bare even on the dirt of the parking lot. In this place where the local men wore jeans and long-sleeved shirts through the September heat, she attracted attention. Guys in the shop turned their heads as if they were mounted on swivels. "Time to roll, buddy!"

"Duty calls, Tazlina. Can't keep Belinda waiting, or I'll hear about it for weeks. She's the beauty, I'm the brawn. I'll swing by on my way back through."

He dragged himself to his feet with a groan. "Arthritis, lower spine," he said, counting his ailments on his fingers. "Bursitis, right elbow. Left's not much better. Hip aches at night on that sleeping pad. Sore rotator cuffs, both of 'em. I'll tell you what, girl, don't ever get old."

"Why do you still do it? You know there might not even be a treasure. It could all be made up."

"I love it," he said, and grinned. "Tougher than all get out, but it's the best feeling in the world. It's mostly about the hunt, you know. Just as good as the finding.

He tipped his hat. "Thanks, girl. Put this on my tab, I'll pay you back."

She watched her father climb laboriously into his pickup and drive away. Missing pistons, she thought. Needs a tune-up. There were probably many more things wrong with that old truck that didn't appear obvious. It was only when you started tearing into it that you would discover all the flaws.

"We have to do something about Dad," her sister always said fiercely on the phone whenever they talked. "He's going to drop dead out there somewhere and nobody's going to know his name."

Lina knew her sister was right. But she also knew that her father would chase the treasure forever, until the mountains were all swept bare by fire, or until arthritis crept so deep into his knuckles it would be impossible to navigate another slope.

At night in their house, before he left the family for the final time, he had spoken of each trip he had loved: hiking down Leslie Gulch to the Owyhee, a flirt of a river, only runnable in spring, no treasure there even though you could hike to a hot spring facing the river edge. The Salmon Breaks, steeper than a man could walk in places, fickle with its enticing canyons. The Green River, where he had flipped an inflatable kayak and been pinned down by current until a friend had grabbed his arm and pulled him out, barely breathing, a close one.

It wasn't just the treasure, he tried to explain. It was the tribe that went with them, irreverent colorful men who played guitars on sandy river bars and lithe women in braids and Carhartts who sang along in reedy soprano. People different than they were. People better than they were, Lina always thought.

She stood for a moment watching the sun glint on the back of his distant pickup. It seemed like there had been a subtle shift in the air, something that felt dangerous and unknown.

Two

Late at night, the twins still awake, their house all that kept them from the unknown wilderness. Lina could feel it right outside the walls, trees scraping the windows like fingernails, mountains—where people got lost and never came back—hemming them in without a clear view of the entire sky.

"Out of all the places on the planet, I can't believe we ended up here," Rainy whispered, their breath and hair mingled together on a single pillow.

"It was for you girls that we moved here," Lina hissed back in a high-pitched imitation of their mother, Liza. "You should be thankful."

Rainy attempted a deep baritone, playing the role of their father. "Liza, the girls are falling in with a bad crowd," she intoned, both trying to muffle laughter. "All those dark clothes. And who knows what else? Reefer madness!"

Lina laughed harder, even though she knew that there had been some truth to the accusations. She and Rainy had indeed been going down what their parents dubbed the wrong path, guided by coral-lipped girls with flasks in their pockets, coming home smelling of strange smoke and freedom. Just say no to drugs, go to the wilderness instead, their parents had said. The wilderness would change them, would turn them into women.

"I miss Salt Lake," Rainy said. She twisted her copper hair into a knot.

"Me too," Lina agreed. She missed the roller-skating rink, "Footloose" blaring over the sound system, her denim-clad legs scissoring around the turns, teetering on the edge between control and falling. She missed her friends, rebellious Mormon girls seduced by her non-belief and the promise of waiting outside a Seven Eleven for strangers to buy them fifths of vodka that burned their throats. She longed for the abandoned quarry down by the railroad tracks, the dizzying launch of the rope swing, the two of them, Rainy and Lina, on one dive, the two of them together, always. She wanted malls with stores and craved the food she couldn't get: Arby's sandwiches, ice cream cones from Dairy Queen, fresh fruit, the juice running down her chin.

"Girls!" their father called from below. "Come look at the maps."

"Dane," they heard their mother snap. "They've seen the maps. Let them be."

"Goddamn maps," Lina grumbled. She sat up and stared out the window as if the view would have changed. No, it was the same as it had been for six agonizing months.

To Lina's eyes, the mountains constantly fought for space, shouldering each other aside as if in battle. They marched, impenetrable and dark-skinned, as far as she could see. They hid the storms until they boiled up over the ridges, a tidal wave of purple-bellied clouds erasing the trees. The mountains betrayed her in that way, luring her with sunny day promise, only to realize, too late, she had been tricked again.

Lina hated the mountains, almost as much as the stupid town of Yellow River Valley.

At least where they lived, her family was in the clear, the sun shining only for them. Anyone could live in town, with its perpetually smoky one-room bar and pizza place combined. The Mercantile, with expired packages of American cheese and equally suspect milk. With goddamn mail delivery, her father said. Instead, they were pioneers, homesteaders. The last of the back to landers. The rest of the hippies, he said, had cashed it in, gotten soft. Not them.

Somehow, they made it through the longest winter Lina had ever known, the town under a thick layer of woodsmoke lying like a grey woolen blanket over the river.

According to Lina's father, Yellow River Valley—which locals called "The Valley"—was named after the water that traversed it, water that would eventually end up in the Snake, which in turn drained into the Columbia. The spring water Lina drank percolated through the thick soil and trickled into that same river. She wasn't impressed.

Her father, on the other hand, boasted that this narrow slice of flat sagebrush paralleled by two mountain ranges—the Chalk and the Isolations—was wondrous.

As far as Lina could tell, nobody went into the Isolations. The tourists spent their time in the more picturesque Chalks, where a wilderness designation had watered the forest down to a series of well-marked and trampled paths that led to scooped-out basins containing lakes that sparkled in the benevolent sun. Just the same, winter came early to the Chalks, and the tourists scattered.

She could feel the tension stretching like a thick band through the house, and without saying it, she knew Rainy could too. She knew also that it was their job to dispel that tension, so she got up and padded down the steps to where her father stood, bent over an enormous map that took up the whole rough-hewn kitchen table.

His thick finger traced the boundary of the Isolations, that wild mountain range to their north. "That's where the action used to be," he said, acknowledging Lina as she hung over his shoulder. "I've heard that in the old days, Basque sheepherders trailed their flocks up to the alpine meadows, so there are probably old trails up there, but they're gone now. Vanished. An old man couldn't possibly make his way up there to hide a treasure. Why waste time looking? Right, Tazlina?"

A knot coiled in her stomach. Lina had thought that moving here would change him, smooth out his rough edges and he would become a real father, not a man with the desire for the hunt chipping away at him in small pieces. Before they moved, he had been satisfied with short stints: a week there, two weeks here. Now, with a job that consisted of explaining invisible things; atoms, molecules, to kids who only understood the tangible day after day, he paced. He set half-full coffee cups on every surface and made new ones.

"Oh, for god's sake, Dane," her mother said from the corner chair. She had not lit the lamp, and her face was in darkness, but Lina heard the clink of ice cubes in a chunky glass. She locked eyes with Rainy, leaning on the loft railing. They didn't even need to speak; Lina could tell what her sister was thinking. *Is he talking about leaving again? What will happen to us then?*

"Just one trip, Liza," her father said, apparently unaware he had said the exact same thing in the past. "I think I have a good lead on it this time. Just one more time and I'll call it."

The stove crackled, drowning out anything her mother might

have said. Lina knew this was their last chance as a family. Back in Salt Lake, there had been fights that spilled out from her parents' room and down the hallway, doors slamming in the middle of the night—*I can't take this anymore, this is all your fault, it's time you grew up.*

Dane and Liza had sat Lina and her sister down and made promises. They had said that this escape to a place above seven thousand feet would change everything. Her mother would stay home and bake cakes that were lighter than air; she would be the compass to get Lina and Rainy back on track. Her father would buckle down and hold a job. They would both change into responsible adults. There were times when Lina thought it was working, nights when her parents sat close together on the front deck as the light began to dim behind the peaks. But after six months of living in Yellow River Valley she knew the experiment had failed.

Her parents were talking low and insistently, forgetting all about Lina.

"Dane. There's nowhere left for us to go. Nobody is going to hire you with your history. You can't throw all this away on a poem written by a senile old man."

"You don't understand, Liza. These kids, they don't want to learn about rocks, or water, or the moon. Ask the girls. All they do is pass notes or stare out the window. On any given day, half don't show up. It's killing me. I'm not a high school science teacher, I'm an adventurer."

"You lost the past three jobs," she said. "You lost them because you did what you always do. Throwing the books out the window, teaching what you think they should know instead of what the school says you should teach. Not showing up because you had a good lead on the treasure. You're lucky someone else would take you."

"Liza. I wasn't accused of anything. It was an overreaction. I was only trying to help the kids understand that there's more than what the government wants them to know. They gave me a big enough severance so that we could buy this place. They just wanted me to go away and not fight it. Who do you believe, me or the bureaucracy?" He straightened up and slammed out of the house, a billow of cold air freezing Lina to the core.

Her mother stood up and crossed angrily to the kitchen. Lina heard the refrigerator door creak open.

"I'm sure you hear all about it at school," she said to Lina. "That he's not the kind of science teacher they expected. That he doesn't stick to the textbooks. That half the time he doesn't show up. Isn't that what they say?"

Lina remembered her father declaring that this school—just like the line of other schools—didn't understand him, that teaching the true story of the age of rocks instead of God was important, the kids deserved to hear both sides.

And, yes, Lina's father had accepted the Yellow River job with reluctance, his wife's ultimatum the final nail. But then some late season treasure hunters had stumbled into the Rod and Gun where he had been nursing a whiskey and a grudge. It was fate. He had been looking for the treasure for years; they spotted a kindred spirit in him. Frostbitten and foot-sore, they had filled him in on another chance, a possibility, places he hadn't thought of looking.

Somehow, he hung onto the teaching job, but Lina knew it wouldn't be long; always leaving for something, anything else. The excuses piled up like snow in the valley.

"I sure hope your father is over the flu soon," Mrs. Finnegan called after Lina in the hallway at school. "He's been out for weeks, the poor man."

"So sorry to hear about your grandmother's passing," Mr. Donegal confided while she played volleyball in PE. "We look forward to having your father back with us when he finishes the funeral arrangements. Why exactly aren't you two back in Boston with him?"

That was the year Lina learned how to lie.

Her mother came out from the kitchen and sat at the table, head in her hands. "We didn't use to be like this," she said. "We were revolutionaries. We were going to change the world. I've told you the stories, haven't I?"

Lina caught a glimpse of Rainy escaping up the stairs. It was too late for her; she was trapped. She stood on one foot, waiting for an out.

"We marched against the war when you two were only toddlers. Chained ourselves to bulldozers over in the redwood country, even lived for a time in a commune outside of Eugene. But that kind of life can't last forever. He thinks he's still like that. Each job is a chance to inflame students, and every time the school board comes down hard."

Liza looked at her daughter between sips. "I've heard people in town talking already. The sandals, the attitude, the Hawaiian shirts. They'll be gone before the end of winter, they're all saying."

"They call us the city twins," Lina said, offering this up as a gift to her mother. An escape route, she thought, a way they could leave for someplace softer. If Lina and Rainy had enough of a difficult time, that could be the excuse to go. She thought of the way the farm kids said it, spitting that name as if it left a bad taste in their mouths. Surely, the city twins would never last. At those times, surrounded by kids so different than she was, she and Rainy would hatch a plan. They would run away, catch a lift with a rancher, head to a place where they weren't surrounded by snowbanks higher than their heads in February, where the snow gushed out of the sky and didn't stop until June. Lina would look at her sister, the same green eyes and copper hair and freckles as she knew she had. At least I have Rainy, Lina would think.

"The people here aren't like us," Lina went on when her mother didn't speak. "They make fun of our clothes, our hair."

Lina understood that her classmates had known each other forever, formed alliances since kindergarten. There was no line between them and wilderness. They told stories of dipping their feet in the nameless creeks that came from springs high on the aspen flank of Carefree Basin. They traveled the tourist trails in the Chalk Wilderness that wound around the mountains like an embrace, climbing so high they could see the whole town, bumming bacon and cookies from the backpackers. They spent nights out wrapped in scratchy wool blankets, hunched over small warming fires. Cowboy camping, they called it, as if that were the only way to sleep. She and Rainy would never, ever fit in.

"Jails and graveyards are full of pretty girls," her mother said dismissively. Lina sighed. Her mother was so far from being young, what did she know? Lina and Rainy wanted what all fifteen-year-old girls wanted, to walk big in a world that wouldn't let them. Legs bronzed under their Levi cut-offs; red bandannas wound around their long and shiny hair, no Dorothy Hamill wedge for them. They were lightning in a bottle, tinder waiting for a match. She felt it sometimes, a pulse, a sizzle in the air.

❖ ❖ ❖

Every day in the winter, Lina and Rainy trudged to school, the wind breathing ice as it pushed through the vacant streets. It got cold, too cold to snow sometimes. Just walking up the half-mile road to their house coated Lina's hair and eyelashes in a frosting of white, her crowded mind ever aware the blood in someone's body could freeze in seconds.

Their father didn't start talking about the treasure again until the air warmed. It had been long enough for complacency, as if he had forgotten about it entirely.

He hadn't. And that summer wasn't easy. There was no transition to the season. Spring was lost; one day the sun broke free and decided to shine. The rivers swallowed the snowmelt and cursed the banks that held them, escaping where they could, gulping big chunks of land as they went. Water spread over the flatlands. So high in elevation, tender white skins began to burn immediately, the forest floor crisping under Lina's feet.

And then came the fires, roaring like dragons in the hills, smokejumpers plummeting from the sky, their canopies looking like jellyfish in a hard-blue sea.

"Still," the people in town would predict, "there could always be a next time; the Big One."

They almost seemed to relish the thought, praising themselves for being so tough to live in such a hard place.

"Wasn't like this in Salt Lake, was it?" they would ask, knowing the answer.

That summer, Lina's father left and didn't come back. That was the summer her mother fell in love with the sun. She offered herself up to it, gave in completely. She stripped down to a high-waisted bikini bottom and strapless top, and lubed herself up with Hawaiian Tropic tanning oil, closing her eyes as if she could erase everything she didn't love: the towering trees that blocked her light, irritating bugs at sundown, her family.

All three reacted in different ways to Dane's absence.

Rainy began a slow retreat down to Yellow River, finding friends in the daughters of ranchers, girls who seemed to thrive on riding horses and a daily dose of chores.

That didn't work for Lina. She was left to follow her own uncertain map, hoping that she could somehow absorb herself into a strange landscape.

Three

At night, when she couldn't sleep, when the wind blew, Lina often thought of those distant days. If she wanted, if she were brave enough, she could climb the crumbling switchbacks on an old horse trail up to Lookout Saddle, a narrow, flat tabletop with ridges stretching in both directions. There she could look across the great gaping mouth of Hells Canyon into Idaho and watch the Seven Devils catch the clouds just across the Snake River. Beyond that, farther than she could see, were the mountains surrounding Yellow River Valley, the place she had lived for only a year.

When she let herself, Lina thought about the hidden trails near her old home, the ones only the three of them had walked. Had the tourists found them, stepped over all the waterbars she had dug? Had they made it to the Floor? Did the Floor still exist or had the fire erased all signs of it, and the notion that anyone had ever been there?

Even though she could picture it in her mind as though she had never left, that place was lost forever ... like trying to imagine the girl she used to be.

Now, standing outside the auto shop in the late summer wind, Lina saw only the years—hair thick as a rope, strands in the copper turning the color of stars, body bundled in too many layers for the season, a woman who had spent too much of her life in hiding. A woman in exile.

She had gotten used to being alone, except for the times when Joe was in town. The guys at the shop would share their Doritos and sorrows, failed marriages, wives who grew tired of the isolation, kids who left town as soon as they could. But at quitting time they beelined it to their pickups, the fog from the diesel hanging like smoke in the still air.

❖ ❖ ❖

Lina had been named for one of the rivers her parents used to run, the Tazlina, up in Alaska.

"It is a sweetheart of a river," her father had said. "Comes out of a lake by the same name and makes its way down to the Richardson Highway." He traced an imaginary line across the table. "The water comes straight out of a glacier. Ends up as a tributary to one of the greatest rivers of all, the Copper." His dark eyes gleamed in the light of the wood stove. "The Copper River, almost three hundred miles long. It doesn't stop until it reaches the Gulf of Alaska."

Lina wasn't sure about being named after a river that was swallowed by another, but she knew she was lucky: he got to name one of the twins, and her mother the other. That was how her sister ended up with their dead grandmother's name, the truly dreadful Lorraine.

Back then she thought it made her special, to have a name so wild and different than anyone else, as if she herself could be that way. What it really meant, she had learned, was that their parents had chosen their favorites: Rainy was the one to sit close to Liza and listen wide-eyed to stories of protest marches and long-haired revolutionaries, and Lina was the one Dane picked to pore over ancient maps and the mysterious poem about a treasure. We love you equally, her parents used to say, but she knew they were wrong. Nothing could ever be quite the same.

It was hard to imagine her mother as a river runner, as an athlete of any kind. According to Liza, a woman could reinvent herself. Women, in fact, she said, were compelled to reinvent themselves, while men could just stroll along being the same old person they had always been. It was the women who had to bend, who had to change, she said, bitter as the taste of acorns.

Lina winced, the memory of her mother rushing into her mind, unannounced, an anxious addition to her growing list of fears. The forked tongue of lightning up high with thunder following. Too much winter rain melting the snowpack and sending floodwaters down the canyon, bridges washing out, houses underwater. The tentacles of the summer sun brewing a melanoma cocktail under her skin. Her mother's bones in strange ground, far from any place she had ever loved.

"This is your fault," Rainy had said at the funeral. "What you did in those mountains killed."

"She was already sick," Lina scolded. "I didn't give her cancer."

"Maybe leaving the valley was what made her die," Rainy lashed back, her words lingering in the hushed silence. "You did this to her."

"She hated Yellow River," Lina argued. "I didn't make her leave."

"Basically, the town threw us out," Rainy snapped. "The hang-up phone calls, people always watching us, talking under their breath when they saw us. Even refusing to serve us in the store. In school that year, the other kids freezing me out, except for Danny. How could we stay?"

Strangers stared as they fought, tossing harsh words between each other like softballs, words they could not take back or would ever forget, coloring every conversation they had had since then.

Only twins could be so close and so separate, their DNA the same but their hearts so closed to each other.

Four

Walking into the shop, she nearly tripped over Ben, who was lying under a Volvo. "Hey, watch it," he protested. "Who just yanked your chain?"

Jimmy came over. He spit on the concrete floor. "Your old man, right? Still hunting up that damn treasure?"

Ben rolled out from under the Volvo, oily rags in hand. "What treasure?"

She had been explaining her father for years and had it down to one or two spare sentences. "Some man named Hunter Malone claimed to have hidden a treasure chest in the mountains, though nobody knows where. Could be New Mexico, could be Montana. He wrote a poem that has clues to where it is. Or so he says."

"Whoa," Ben said. He was a coltish twenty-one, still believing in miracles. "Why isn't everyone looking for it?"

"Because it doesn't exist," Lina sighed. "There's a whole tribe of people who think it does. They've died looking for it, by drowning or falling from a mountain. My father's obsessed with it. He's been looking for it most of my life."

Ben stared out at the place where Dane had been. "But maybe there really is a treasure," he said. "Wouldn't that be great if there was?"

Jimmy snapped a grimy towel in his direction. "And wolves are swimming the Snake to attack Oregon," he said. "Now get back to work. I don't pay you to daydream."

"I want to see that poem," Ben said under his breath before rolling back under the vehicle. Automatically Lina picked up a service slip: Bronco, new steering fluid. She could do that in her sleep.

The postcard crinkled in her pocket and, curious, she pulled it out. On the front, the iconic shot of Yellow River Valley, the Chalk Mountains forming a craggy spine above the flat valley, the oxbow where the river had changed its mind and decided to abandon its former course. A bluebird August day. On the back, a few scrawled words:

> *Dear Tag,*
> *Hope life is glorious and you're still working the*
> *trails up to the Floor. Remember to fly.*
> *Cassie*

Lina bent over as if kicked in the stomach, remembering that last moment, Cassie's hair a halo of flame. Once again, Lina's desperate fingers reaching for Cassie's coat, sparks spitting over her head and catching fire in front of her. The one thought in Lina's head—run as fast as you can. Lina pictured herself running down the mountain, afraid to look back, praying that Cassie was on her heels.

How could it be? She looked up to see Jimmy eyeing her quizzically.

"Bad news?" he asked.

Lina shook her head, tucking the card back in her pocket, her heart attempting to explode through her skin.

Numb, she went back to work.

❖ ❖ ❖

Driving back up Starvation Road, Lina allowed herself to imagine that Joe was there, waiting for her, a beer in one hand and a fishing rod in the other. "Let's go over to the river," he would say. They would slide themselves as slow as summer into water that stole their breath, water that had only been ice a few weeks before. She would forget all about Cassie, and Idaho, and the time before.

Or maybe she would talk to Joe. Really talk to someone for the first time since the Bad Place. She would tell him about Rainy, about the summer they had fractured apart. The summer her father left, and her mother lost herself to the sun. The summer of fire.

❖ ❖ ❖

An aimless wind blew the curtains as Lina climbed the steps. She gulped down the bile that rose in her throat. Joe was not there.

Strangely quiet, she thought. Joe could burst the small cabin at its seams with his laughter. Instead, there was only the breeze, sighing around the dilapidated boards.

The hippies who had built the cabin—displaced mariners—had turned it into the replica of a small ship with hooks for clothes, shelves up and down the slanted walls, a porthole for a window. They had only lasted landlocked for a few years before they fled for the sea, leaving a clandestine marijuana garden and the place in shambles. On the nights when the wind blew, Lina often imagined she was on a ship after all, Hells Canyon now lost beneath the ocean.

❖ ❖ ❖

Unable to find Joe, Lina returned inside, letting the screen door slam behind her, as loud as a gunshot in the still afternoon. Dust motes rose lazily in the sunlit room. The place was undisturbed, the way she had left it.

Lina palmed the phone and dialed the far-away number. Her sister would answer; she always did.

"Rainy, hi." Lina heard her sister breathe. Impatient? Annoyed? Rainy always seemed to have that reaction.

"Lina, what is it? I don't really have time to talk. We're getting ready for a hurricane here. It's not the season, so I don't know what the hell this is, but they're calling it a hurricane. Don't you watch the news? Category three and getting bigger. Landfall tonight. We've got supplies and we're putting plywood on the windows. ... Danny, that's not where that goes!"

Lina imagined hapless Danny, staggering under the weight of one of Rainy's garden statues.

"Rainy, this is important. Dad came by."

"Better you than me. What did he want this time? Let me guess. A bit short on cash. Needs some to tide him over until he finds the treasure."

"It's not that. Well, it is, but that's not why I'm calling. He said he went through the valley. Rainy, Silas was there. He's moved back."

"Oh, for Pete's sake, Lina. It was one summer. You need to let it go."

There was a silence, deep with all the things neither of them could say.

"Rainy, that's not everything. I got a postcard. A postcard from Cassie."

Outside Lina's open window the birds had all gone silent. A mountain lion skirting the edges of the property? A bear bumbling downslope? A sharp-shinned hawk looking for dinner.

There was plenty of noise on the other end of the phone: the sound of a hammer, a deep sigh.

"What do you mean, a postcard from Cassie? I know you don't want to believe it, Lina, but Cassie's dead. She died that day. You know that. If someone sent you a postcard, it wasn't Cassie."

"But what if it was? What if she's alive?"

"Remember the fire, Lina? Remember how it burned? You saw it. There's no way she could have survived. I told you, someone's pulling a prank."

Silence.

"Lina," Rainy continued, "every few days you call up wanting to know what to do about Joe, should you move somewhere else, should you give Dad money. I can't keep telling you what to do with your life."

"Rainy, this is different."

"Look, Lina. I get it, I really do. You made a bad decision years ago to follow that girl up the mountain. Then you paid for it. But it's time to get over it. It happened, it's over."

"I need to know what Silas knows," Lina insisted. "He might know something about what happened. About where she is."

An exasperated sigh. "They'll run you out of that valley, Lina. I wouldn't go back in a million years. Don't you remember what you went through? What I went through?"

"They might have forgotten." The minute she said it, Lina

knew how foolish that sounded.

"Yellow River people don't forget," Rainy stated flatly. "None of us will ever forget."

"I haven't forgotten," Lina said. "But by now the forest has come back. People have other things to think about."

Surely that was true. Each season made loss less sharp. Most people had rebuilt. Others had moved away; some had died. Could anyone hold a grudge for fifteen years?

"Why should anyone have believed you," Rainy said. "You were up there too. You could have stopped her."

The hammering of plywood increased in intensity.

"Wind is picking up," Rainy added. "We're seeing the first bands. We'll probably lose power soon. I'd better go help him and make sure the kids didn't sneak down to the beach to watch the waves. I swear, those two. Sometimes I think they should have been twins, as close as they are. Mom was right about being cursed with having kids like we were."

There wasn't anything left to say. There never was with Rainy. Her sister was decisive, unlike Lina. Rainy latched onto a thought or an idea and never wavered.

"Listen," Rainy said. "I'm not going to tell you what to do. But nothing good can come out of going back there. We were kicked out of the valley and told never to come back. People remember. Ask Danny. If he even sees smoke, he has nightmares. It's not something you ever forget."

What makes you think Silas is going to want to see you, anyway?" Rainy continued. "For all you know he blames you for what happened to Cassie. Those social workers hustled him out of town so fast after it happened that none of us ever got to say goodbye. Not that we really would have, you know. None of us were very nice to him. Remember how we called him Bullet? I can't even remember why we called him that."

"Carried a pellet gun around," Lina heard Danny shout in the background. "Weirdo. Come on, Lor, I could use a hand here."

"Lina, this time I really have to hang up. But listen. I'm making some changes. I'm taking time for me. With the kids, and with my real estate business the way it is, in a deep dive, I don't have time to be your therapist. You need to start living your life, do you hear me? There's more to life than working in an auto shop, holing up in the mountains. Promise me you'll think about moving ... maybe coming here."

"Lorraine," Lina heard Danny call. She knew what he was thinking. The sister who had started all the trouble. The reason his parents fled, their house in ashes. Lina could still picture them sifting through cooling timbers, trying to find something, anything, that remained of their old life.

"Rainy, Danny's not going to want me there."

"Well, me and him, we need to have a come to Jesus meeting one of these days. He'll cave. He always does. I really have to go. We'll probably lose power again, so don't bother calling for a few days, a week maybe." Rainy paused as if she were deciding whether to say anything more. Then, "That girl had a death wish from day one. I never understood what you saw in those two. She could have killed you that night. I tried to tell you. There was something not quite right about any of them. All you had to do was look in their eyes. They weren't normal."

"Normal might be underrated," Lina said, feeling as though she might laugh, as if it were bubbling up from under her skin.

"Lina, none of that matters anymore. She's gone and you need to move on. Going back there makes no sense. And, by the way, we need to get Dad to sell the place for once and for all. He's never going to live there again. None of us are. Why would we, for God's sake?"

❖ ❖ ❖

Lina walked in bare feet onto the deck. The birds had started singing again, tentative chirps against the growing darkness. Foolish birds. Didn't they know that the moment they let their guard down was the most dangerous time?

When she and Rainy were fifteen, barely into the summer that would break them apart, Lina had figured that they would grow up within a breath of each other. They would live on the same street in houses that had gates that swung onto each other's backyards. They had sworn they would never marry, but if they ever did, they would marry brothers, twins ... only twins could know each other down to the bones the way she and Rainy did. When it all changed, it was as deep a betrayal as Lina could imagine.

A glass of whiskey in hand, Lina sat down on the rough-cut steps made from left-over lumber pallets. This deep inside the mountains, backed right up to the mouth of Hells Canyon, she was protected.

Without thought, Lina tossed her whiskey off the porch, showering the dead grass below. Silas was back. She shivered as the wind made its way up the slope.

❖ ❖ ❖

Late that night, Lina could not sleep, her mind racing the wind as it pooled off the mountains and down the valley.

Rainy had to be right. Lina had seen the mountain explode into flame. She had barely made it out herself. Nobody farther up the mountain could have escaped. The postcard was a joke, someone trying to make trouble, that was all it was.

"Cassie," she whispered. "Are you alive?"

There was no answer, not here. It would be somewhere else, a place where she had been told to never return. A place where fear would consume her like fire ... or finally let her go.

Five

One thing every fifteen-year-old girl could agree on ... Tony Ray was a fox.

His hair, the color of a new fawn, was feathered back from his narrow face and brushed his shoulders, just like Shaun Cassidy's. He strutted through school in his corduroy pants, an entirely different creature than the farm kids, even though he was technically one of them. All the girls were mesmerized, and he knew it. Only Rainy seemed immune to his charms.

"I'm getting a keg," Tony Ray said in typing class when Mr. Smith, the teacher, lurked in another part of the room, explaining the proper use of white-out. Even though it was the last day of school, Mr. Smith was a stickler, ignoring the heat that crept in through the single-paned windows and the feeling of imminent freedom that intoxicated everyone.

It was a small school, all the ninth-grade kids in the same classes. Lina sat next to Rainy by virtue of the alphabet, eyes on their separate typewriters. Tony Ray sat in front of them. Lina had spent many hours noticing how the point of his hair brushed his shoulders, but this was the first time he had spoken to her directly. "Check it, it's an eight gallon and I'm only inviting eight people. That way we all get our share. Down at the Boatman's Box, after dark. You two want in?"

"He's such a loser," Rainy said under her breath. "Tony Ray. As if."

The sound of clacking keys and hard returns covered her words. "What was that?" Tony Ray glowered. "Come on. We need some cute bitches at this party. Nothing else is going on in this town. What do you say?"

Danny leaned over from his typewriter. "I'm going," he said to Rainy. There wasn't anything special that Lina could see about Danny. He was just another one of the band geeks, indistinguishable except for the giant tuba he hauled down the halls. Danny was so invisible and inoffensive that everybody liked him. He moved between social levels easily, as though he were simply climbing a tree.

Lina waited to see what Rainy would say, so she could take her own cue. "Well, I might," Rainy said, surprising Lina.

"Well, you'd better," Danny said. He didn't look at Lina. He had meant his invitation only for Rainy. "I'll be there, and that's enough reason to go."

"I'm so sure," Rainy said, but she smiled and looked down at her typewriter, her hair falling like a curtain, hiding her face.

"Not enough typing over here," Mr. Smith said, glaring in their direction. "Still fifteen minutes before the bell."

"Make sure you show up," Tony Ray said to Lina before swiveling in his chair. "People are calling you weird, stuck up. Prove them wrong. Show up."

Lina knew he was right: it was only a matter of time before she was a target. There were a few of those, friendless kids who wandered like lone wolves down the hallways, moving on diagonals to appear less visible. Groups of kids taunted them with cruel nicknames: Wide Betty, Wussy Charlie. Elaborate jokes were played upon them: fake love letters from a popular girl shoved into lockers, gym shorts swiped and run up the flagpole. The end came in three ways: either a kid bore it stoically, head down, until graduation or until an easier target appeared, the brave ones fought it out, or the kid just vanished from school one day, never to return.

The teachers were never around when any of this occurred, and their outlook was that they all needed to toughen up anyway. The world, they implied, wasn't for the weak. There were droughts that withered all your crops; unexpected rains that spoiled your hay. Men would break your heart; women would leave you for another. School was no different. Sticks and stones, they said if anyone tried to speak up on a kid's behalf. Every kid soon learned that it did no good to tell tales. They learned that it was better to stay out of the crossfire altogether.

Lina had studied the school hierarchy. There were several tiers, and you had to work your way through them. Most kids got stuck on one and stayed there forever. It was difficult to skip a rung. First there were the jocks and the cheerleaders, even in their small school. They stuck together, closing ranks against the rest of them. Below them were the shiny, popular kids, and in descending order, the smart kids, the normal kids, and the ones who slipped under the radar. The lowest rung of all were the relentlessly strange, the weird, the outcasts. She had never questioned these layers before. In her old school, it was just the way it was, and she had floated to the top easily by virtue of being a standout, a redhead among blondes, slightly dangerous because her father had denounced religion in a state that was seeped in it. Now she wondered: who made up the rules? Who got to decide who was on top and who sunk to the bottom?

Lina stole a glance at Rainy. She had tucked her hair behind her ears and was typing studiously.

Until now, everyone had included both of them in invitations. It was a given. You invited one, you included the other, a matched set. But now they weren't a matched set. Rainy had cut her hair into a Marie Osmond bob. She had joined band. When Lina asked why, Rainy wrinkled her nose. "Just because we have the same DNA doesn't mean we have to like the same things," she said. "I'm tired of people comparing us, or worse, lumping us into one category. The twins this, the twins that. I'm over it."

Lina thought that she could see into the future, a future where she no longer saw Rainy every day, a world she would have to brave on her own. Her sister had always been her compass. If she were unsure, Lina would look to Rainy, and the opposite was also true. Now Rainy was turning into a stranger, leaving Lina behind.

"Jails and graveyards are full of pretty girls," their mother said that night, watching Lina and Rainy make up their faces to look like women. "Pretty isn't everything, you know."

But it was. At fifteen, being pretty was the only thing that mattered.

After Dane had left, their mother had changed.

"What's up with her?" Lina whispered as she and Rainy curled their hair in the bathroom. "She keeps following us around."

"She's crazy," Rainy said. "She still thinks he'll come back after the summer ends."

"He'll come home soon," Lina said, dusting bronzer on nonexistent cheekbones, trying to shape her face into something it wasn't. She knew her words were as useless as the bronzer. Both of them knew their father was lost to them.

"As if," Rainy answered. She sat on the closed toilet seat and flipped through a magazine. "He won't come back until there's no treasure left to find."

❖ ❖ ❖

Lina and Rainy stepped into Molly's waiting car, driven by her older brother Ned. The aroma of Loves Baby Soft choked the air and Ned rolled down the window in disgust. He had been pressed into service with promises of free beer, and he hunched impatiently over the wheel of the family station wagon, wanting to ditch his cargo as soon as possible.

Lina hesitated, half in the car and half out. From the curtainless windows she could see her mother in her leotard and leg warmers, stretching her arms high over her head. As much as Lina wanted to escape the perpetual darkness of the house, it was safe there. She knew what to expect. There would be hot tea, and the three of them in terrycloth robes, brushing past each other to brush their teeth, the hum of three women breathing in sleep.

But there was Rainy, in hoop earrings that brushed her shoulders, her eyes bright with anticipation, and Rainy wanted Lina to go with her.

"But don't hang around with me the whole time," Rainy warned. "Danny's going to be there, and I don't need a third wheel. You can't ruin this for me, Lina. He's the first boy who's ever liked me."

"Hey, what's the holdup?" Ned scolded. "Let's motor. I'm

hoping to get lucky tonight."

"Gross," Molly said.

Rainy reached over Lina and pulled the door shut with a finality that made the decision for her. They drove down the road and into the waiting night.

❖ ❖ ❖

The party showed no signs of abating. Below it, the Yellow River was a crumpled silver blanket in the moonlight that filtered in from above low-hanging clouds. Lina clung in her unsuitable heels to the unstable grassy slopes, drinking bitter beer with too much foam. The others were dark shapes as they flitted around the clearing. Most of them were older boys, she didn't know them, friends of Tony Ray's from California that he had met when they came up with their families to camp one summer. They mostly ignored her, diving into the river and then dropping into the wooden tub that collected hot water out of a pipe, their boxer shorts hung low over narrow hips. Blue Oyster Cult played at a volume that was not loud enough to attract passing cops. Don't fear the reaper, the boys sang. Baby, I'm your man.

Steam from the hot springs swirled over the party like fog. The keg sat in the back of someone's pickup, and two boys obligingly pumped it whenever she approached with an empty Solo cup. "Chug!" they urged each other. One of them swore he was going to swim across the river and back if enough of them put up money to see it. When nobody did, he swam anyway, emerging red-faced and victorious.

"This party bites," Rainy said. "Danny isn't even here. These guys are losers. I'm blowing this popsicle stand."

"We can't leave," Lina said. "How are will we get home? Last I saw Molly she was heading into the woods with some boy whose name she doesn't even know. And Ned, our designated driver, was doing multiple keg stands. By now, he's probably passed out in the weeds."

"We can hitch," Rainy said. "It's Friday night. Plenty of cowboys heading to town."

The town went dark at the same time as the sky. There was nothing for them in town. There was only this, the dangerous undercurrent of the river, the occasional burst of a firework, set off by boys who were not boys or men, but something in between.

"I want to stay," Lina said. She couldn't face their house, empty except for their mother, depending on her mood either shuffling around in her sheepskin slippers or stepping up and down on an exercise box in time to a workout tape, either way a deep sadness that was almost thick enough to smell.

Rainy peered at her through the darkness. "Seriously? You're not going to come with?"

She waited for Lina to do what she always did, follow her. When Lina didn't, Rainy threw her cup and they watched it fall in a long arc to the bushes. "Suit yourself. I'm out of here."

"You can't go by yourself," Lina said. "Remember Heartbreak Creek Helen!"

"I'm not scared," Rainy said. "That was way back in the winter. Old news."

"Nobody was ever caught. Her murderer could be driving down the highway right now."

"Don't be stupid," Rainy snapped. "Dad said she wasn't from here. Whoever dumped her in Heartbreak Creek is miles away now."

Lina shivered. She thought about Heartbreak Creek Helen and the artist drawings of her, a small tattoo of a yellow, red, and black banded snake curling over her left shoulder, a name inked into her skin below it. Long straw-colored hair flowing in a cold current.

"Do what you want. I'm leaving." Rainy turned and began climbing the steep, muddy path to the highway.

"Don't go," Lina called, but Rainy stuck her thumb out to a passing pickup. Its headlights lit her whole body up, the long sweep of her ponytail, the silky fabric of her jacket.

The truck stopped and she got in. She didn't even look back, not once.

Lina stomped angrily down into the light and heat of the party, the exaggerated shrieks, the flames of the bonfire.

Six

Three times Lina had thrown a backpack and a pair of boots into the back seat of the Bronco. Three times she had taken them out. She picked up the phone to call Rainy and then set it down without dialing. She sat in the car for a long time, listening to the hum of the engine. There were no indications of any trouble: broken sway bar, busted ball joints. No reason not to go. A lot of reasons to stay. She hit the steering wheel. "Just drive, Tazlina," she said.

Lina steered the car down Starvation Road and hit the brakes in front of Lucy's place, noting the slight hitch in the old woman's stride as she came up to her window. Lucy never complained about weakness or pain, so Lina didn't mention it.

"Come in for a few minutes?" Lucy asked. "I have iced tea." Lina realized for the first time that Lucy might be lonely, living the last decades of her life alone on the river, her husband long in the little cemetery up valley. But she shoved that thought away. Lucy had plenty of friends.

"I'll be away for a few days," Lina said. "Could you tell Joe when he comes back?"

If Lucy was disappointed, she didn't show it. "Sure thing, honey. Come in next time." Lucy stepped back as Lina eased on the gas. "Be careful on the Kleinschmidt Grade."

Lina looked through the rearview. Lucy was already bent over her tomatoes, pulling weeds. A prickle of unease started low in her stomach. How did Lucy know she was headed east, over the washboards and steep switchbacks leading out of Hells Canyon? From here, she could have been going anywhere: south to the Nevada desert, west to the coast. What did Lucy know?

She couldn't think about that now, her entire focus on the road. Just like everything else, the driving here wasn't easy. When she left the good gravel, it was a steep, treacherous freefall down to the Snake River, tough on brakes and nerves. Then the road rocketed back up again, headed straight for the sky. There was barely enough room for two vehicles to pass, and once she had to back up for a horse trailer bound the other way.

Once, this place had felt like the most remote spot on the planet. In coming here, Lina had believed she could erase the past as easily as she had swept the halls of the Bad Place, wielding the dustpan as she gathered everything the other lost girls had dropped or left on purpose. Now she knew she had been wrong.

Be careful on the Kleinschmidt Grade. Too late Lina realized that anyone could hunt her down, even here in the stark, waterless canyons. Her past had come with her, an unwelcome passenger that she couldn't quite jettison.

Lina stopped in a tiny river outpost near Banks to fill up the Bronco. A girl in a Stihl cap and cargo pants came to wash the windshield. "Lot of dust on these roads," she said, spitting her gum on the ground and polishing the glass with a dirty rag slung through a murky pail. "Going up to Yellow River? That's the most beautiful place in the world."

She squinted up at Lina and snapped the windshield wipers back in place. "Big fire came through when I was just a baby, and my parents can't let it go, keep saying it ruined the place, but I think those silver trees are as pretty as can be, especially when the sun catches them. Don't you?"

Lina froze, tugging her own baseball cap lower on her forehead, but the girl didn't seem to expect an answer. "Have a nice day," she chirped, snapping the wet rag in the air to dry it.

❖ ❖ ❖

As the forested two-lane highway unrolled ahead of her, the miles clicking down to the valley, Lina thought about turning around. Why was she doing this? The closer she got, the more dangerous it felt, as though she had crossed an invisible line between safety and the unknown. But as she crested a hill, the slate peaks of the Isolations appeared, piercing the sky in a jagged line. She caught her breath, her foot coming off the gas pedal. She had forgotten this, the way the mountains took up all the space, how they rose abruptly from the sagebrush as though carved out by a saw. There were no soft curves here. The land was tough and sharp, blasted by subzero winds in winter, colonized by hardy plants that only had a few months to grow. It had been shaped by glaciers and looked it; people only able to tame the edges.

A horn blared as a red Blazer hurtled past on a double yellow. Lina saw the angry blur of a face and an upraised finger. The plates were from Washington. Nobody she knew. Increasing her speed slightly, she rolled into town.

She took the last curves slowly, her heart a nervous staccato.

Life wouldn't be worth living unless you were all in, her father had always said. Everything he did was with gusto and flair. He said that there was an edge you could get to if you dared, the edge between desire and catastrophe, where you skated along on one foot, balancing risk and reward. Why wouldn't you always want to aim for that edge, he asked her. It was the only thing that fed him. He couldn't understand why everyone else wasn't the same way.

"Scared of something? Just do it scared, then," he had said, winking at her.

The Seven Devils behind her had faded into the horizon as if they had never existed, replaced by an endless forest. Was Joe out there somewhere? He had often said he wanted to pack up two weeks' supplies and head out on foot, across the canyon, swim the river at the Dug Bar crossing the way the Nez Perce had, and keep going until he ran out of mountains. Lina admitted to herself that part of the reason she was driving to the Yellow River Valley was to prove to him that she could be as brave as he was. And maybe to her father as well: she too could skate that edge.

❖ ❖ ❖

Despite what her father had said, much of the place hadn't changed. Travelers still came to it from above, dropping down from a steep grade that required the lowest gear. The road spit her into a hemmed-in valley carpeted with silver sage. In the distance, a bold blue river cut a lazy diagonal. This pocket of land and sky seemed like both a refuge and a prison. One way in, one way out.

She saw that the town had endured, as brash and strong as

it had been before. Buildings built low against the wind lined the street: there was the river rafting company headquarters, on the next corner the laundromat and post office. A band played earnestly on the deck of the Rod and Gun.

The road where Silas and Cassie had lived still curved up toward the Isolations, although she could see a new housing development carved into the hill, maybe the houses her father had mentioned.

She felt eyes on her as she drove through town, slowed by packs of tourists in floppy hats and shorts jaywalking across the street. The growl of her muffler seemed too loud in the mountain air. Who was watching? Who knew she was back? She wheeled onto the old cabin road and away from the main street as quickly as she could.

The road to her old house was the same as before, an unmarked boulder-studded crawl upward, craters where rain had washed out the soil, an ominous thud across the oil pan. The old gate swung open reluctantly with a metallic screech. Nobody had put much effort into the road. The forest was slowly reclaiming it; trees scraped against the doors and deep ruts were etched into the dirt. A few more winters and nobody would be able to drive in anymore.

Over time the carpenter ants and the porcupines had chewed on the house, leaving it with an abandoned air. The trees that now surrounded her had taken over in her absence; their former clearing looked as though it was about to be swallowed whole. Lina shivered a little and hurried to the front door, away from the advancing trees.

The key was still where she remembered, hidden between the door and the frame. Lina swung the screen door open and stepped back into her past. When Rainy and their mother had left, they had fled with only a carload of belongings, only the bare minimum needed to survive. Since then, someone had carted away many of the things they had left. The house was anonymous now, just a series of rooms full of old furniture, permeated with the musty smell of loneliness. The water pump from the spring still worked; it had been wrapped for winter years ago, but there were no lights. Inside, the house lurked in a perpetual dusk.

Upstairs in the loft their twin beds still occupied the small space, stripped down to the frames. Everything she remembered was gone: their matching ballerina jewelry boxes, the clutter of makeup and curling irons with tangled cords, even all their clothes, the open closet empty of anything but a few wire hangers swaying together as she peered in.

Though the house was empty, it seemed packed to the rafters with the people they had been. In her imagination, she could still hear their voices echoing through the rooms. *"You must go,"* her mother had softly whispered, crumbling as though her body were made of dust. *"If you don't, what will become of all of us."* And Rainy, her eyes big as plates. *"Don't leave me here, Lina. We can find somewhere to hide, can't we, until this blows over?"*

Lina gazed around the smoky house. Staying here seemed wrong now, impossible.

But it was late, the sun having dipped well below the trees. Too late to find Silas. Too late to try to find a lonely bed in the one hotel in town. She would have to sleep here.

Lina considered the loft bedroom but discarded the thought. Her parents' room was missing window glass, boarded up with plywood. Finally, she threw out her sleeping bag on the creaky pine floor in the kitchen.

❖ ❖ ❖

Though she didn't expect to sleep at all, the morning light woke her. It slanted warm and hopeful across the dusty floor.

Lina dressed in anonymous clothes: a long-sleeved synthetic button-down, khaki pants, clothes for a hunt. She pulled a baseball cap low over her head and stuffed her tell-tale hair inside. With that and the years that had passed, she was as hidden as she would ever be.

In town, a crush of people already lined the streets even though the chill remained from the night before. River people, backpackers, and sunburnt tourists all mingled together in search of coffee and entertainment. She parked and walked into the post office. "Help you?" an older woman asked. Lina didn't recognize her.

"This postcard. Did someone mail it from here? Do you remember who sent it?"

She flipped it over. "Oh honey, see, it isn't postmarked. So, somebody just addressed it but never stamped or sent it. Looks like they used an address we don't deliver to. Can't get our trucks up there. I've only been here a couple of years, and I don't recall anyone ever living up there. Sorry, don't know what else to tell you."

"Where do people buy these cards?"

"That's a popular one. Maybe check with the Merc?"

In the Merc, the woman at the register sported a buzz cut and rivet-shaped earrings. She shook her head briskly. "So many people come through here," she said. "I don't even look at them, just ring them up and keep the line moving. Not like they're sticking around."

She leaned in with the practiced look of a woman who liked

to gossip. "Sounds like you're looking for someone who might have bought the card. Sorry I can't help you, but I do think I know just about everyone here, if you're trying to find a local."

Lina weighed her options. Her need to find Silas overtook caution. She lowered her voice as a man with a ponytail approached the counter carrying a twelve pack of Bud.

"Silas Van Allen. Do you know him?"

The clerk paused. Something unreadable raced across her tanned face. "Everyone knows him. Keeps to himself, though. Word is he's pretty intense. Strange, you know? Stays up in that subdivision, the one you can see from here. Can't miss it. Sticks out like a sore thumb."

"Thanks," Lina said, but the clerk was already turning away to ring up the order, forgetting her entirely, she hoped.

Lina walked outside ... a small crowd clustered around her Bronco. Locals, all of them.

"I was right, you guys," gloated one of the women, jutting out her chin. Was it Kelly? She looked older, bitter.

Lina swallowed hard. Too late to run.

"You have a lot of nerve," Kelly spat, "coming around here."

Once they had woven each other friendship bracelets, vowing not to take them off their wrists until they rotted. Now, she and two others boxed Lina in where she stood. There was a solid wall of women, all in t-shirts and braids.

"I won't be here long," Lina said. "This doesn't have anything to do with you."

After so many years, how did this feel just like high school? Walking timidly down the halls, the smell of pine cleanser and fear overpowering her. Fear that she would stand out. Fear that something would be wrong with her clothes. Fear of being different.

"I can't believe it," Susan chimed in. She had always been Kelly's sidekick, a rounder, less popular version, imitating Kelly's off-the-shoulder sweatshirts and spiral perm. She looked as though she still copied Kelly, her hair corralled in a side braid, her trucker hat the same brand. "A lot of people are still mad ... we can't be responsible for what might happen if you stick around."

Teenagers during the nights of the orange flame, these women had nursed embers for a decade and a half, unable to forgive.

Molly was the third woman, a thinner version of her fifteen-year-old self, a new worry line etched between her brows, but the same bright hair escaping from her braids. A baby hung from her neck and shoulders, swaddled in a purple scarf.

"Now, guys," she said. "We don't have to be mean. We don't have a problem with you, Lina. But it's probably better if you don't stay."

"I have a problem," Kelly said. The slight pixie with irregularly cut bangs had vanished; she was now a thick woman in bog boots, her body appearing as if it could part the air she walked through. "You were trouble from the minute you landed here. We tried to be your friend and look what you did."

"Come on, Kelly," Molly said, looking straight at Lina without blinking. Overcome with Molly's kindness, Lina managed a nod.

"I don't trust you," Kelly said. "So, tell me. How do you sleep at night after what you did to us?"

"I told the truth," Lina said. She backed up against the Bronco, but the wrong side of it. Where were her keys? Was this how Silas had felt when a gang of boys had surrounded him? "It was an accident, you know that."

"Bull," Kelly said. "You remember how dry it was that summer. They cancelled the fireworks at the lake? The forest was just waiting to burn. All of us could see it. You must have known."

"We had to let our horses go and just pray they would be all right," Susan said. "Didn't even have time to spray paint our phone number on their hooves. We lost everything. My mother never got over it."

"We all never got over it," Kelly agreed.

"It might have been an accident," Molly said.

"Easy for you to stick up for her. Your house didn't even burn."

Molly shrank back, gone from Lina's sight ... her only ally.

Susan pushed forward in anger. "What are you doing here anyway, Lina?"

"You never belonged here in the first place," Kelly said. "I remember you and your sister, thinking you were better than us because you didn't have cow shit on your boots. Stuck-up, I always thought. Your family up there on the hill, never coming down unless you wanted something from one of us."

The tourists walking by gave them a wide berth.

The men spoke up next, shouldering the women aside. They smelled of hay and horses and, unlike the women, pretended to be friendly. Good old boys chewing on toothpicks.

She didn't recognize most of them, but the older one was Leroy Patterson, who had once been a friend of her father's. She remembered him coming to the cabin to drink glasses of amber colored liquid and look at maps. With stubby fingers, Leroy had pointed out where the old gold mines were, where the sheep had used to trail in the wilderness before the enviros had shut that down. Where he and his boys had cut big timber, before that had been shut down too.

"I bet you were just in a situation way over your head," Leroy said now. "Always liked your family, even if your dad was sort of a whack job."

"Your dad was okay," a man in suspenders said. "Does it really matter? Both of them girls were up there. Old enough to know better. Old enough to know what would happen."

Lina suddenly realized the man was Jim Scott. A classmate in high school, he was at least forty extra pounds heavier and had acquired the tomato-colored face of a habitual drinker.

"If Tony Ray catches wind of this, there will be hell to pay," Jim continued. "You never know with him ... he can get serious."

Leroy leaned so close that Lina could smell his chewing gum. Peppermint.

"This is for your own good," Leroy said in a low voice. "Tony and his dad seemed to have it in for you back then. Stomped around town saying you should have gotten jail time. And whatever you do, don't go up in the mountains. We all have a suspicion about what he's doing up there. Consider it a warning, a friendly warning."

The men coughed, looked down at their boots.

Lina knew it wouldn't be that easy. Just her coming here had changed things, opened old scars. It seemed like a sullen mood hung over the valley, like a thunderstorm waiting to break.

"The mountains will never be the same," Leroy said. "Our children, their children's children, nobody will ever know it the way we did. It hurts my heart."

"The trees are coming back," Jim said. "But it's taken a long time. Some of those lakes we used to pack into in the Chalks, there's no good feed there anymore. The fire took the seedbank. Just miles of dead trees."

"They say lodgepole loves fire," Leroy added. "And I guess that's true. Opens the cones, they say. Forest's thicker now than it ever was. Looks good, in places. But still, you and she didn't have the right to play God like that. You should have left it for the lightning."

"Pine beetle came in," Jim said. "Got a foothold after the fire. Finished off a lot of the old trees. Just the young ones are left. Maybe they'll be strong enough."

They looked as though they were near tears. The women next to them shifted uneasily, silent and angry. She scanned their faces. There was nothing soft about them.

Lina swallowed again. The old Lina, the one she had always been, would nod wordlessly, crawl into her Bronco and drive away. But where had that ever gotten her? Hiding up on Starvation Road, at the whim of the wind and her dreams? She knew that she couldn't run away now. She couldn't spend fifteen more years being afraid.

Tazlina, like the river. The Tazlina, born from a glacier, its silty water finally merging with one of the biggest rivers of all, the Copper. *Live up to your name.*

"That's enough," she said, her voice growing stronger as she spoke. "Look at all of you, surrounding me like this. What do you mean to do to me?" She gestured to the busy street. "Plenty of witnesses."

"Whoa there," Leroy said. "Nobody's going to hurt you or nothing like that. Are we?" He looked around the group. Nobody would meet his eyes. "Of course we aren't. Just a lot of strong feelings left over in the valley, that's all."

"There's still something that stinks about this," Kelly piped up. "And Tony Ray's going to want to know. He's day drinking at the Rod and Gun right now. I think I'll just head on down there. If I were you, I'd clear on out."

Kelly turned on her heel and strode down the street toward

the bar. The others followed her, hurrying to keep up. Nobody looked back. They expected her to obey, get in her car and drive away. And why wouldn't they? She had always done what other people had told her to do.

Lina thought Molly had gone, but she came out from where she had retreated under the covered store porch. She looked flustered, her face a storm of emotions. Her baby clung to her, casting suspicious glances in Lina's direction.

"Listen, Lina. This is a small town. All winter long it's only us, then the tourists show up, look right through you like you don't exist, waiting for you to clean up after them. I've known those girls forever. We look after each other. They might be royal bitches, but if I need them, they'd be there to help. You remember how it is here."

She placed a cool hand on Lina's arm. "For what it's worth, I figured that Cassie Van Allen must have really had some demon in her that made her do what she did. I kind of felt sorry for her, to tell the truth."

"She wasn't a bad person. She was..." Lina's throat closed up, the momentary braveness deserting her. How would she ever describe Cassie? "She was glorious," Lina said finally, using Cassie's favorite word.

Molly shrugged. "I hope you find what you're looking for, but I can't figure out why you came back. I never got out of here, not for lack of trying. But the first kid came along and, well, I could never be so brave. If you've got a life somewhere else, you ought to go live it and forget all about this place."

It wasn't bravery, Lina wanted to say. The brave ones had stayed, rebuilt their lives.

Molly sighed. "Kelly and them, they aren't bad people," she said. "I know it doesn't come off that way. They're just tired."

She looked up toward the new houses, looming over town, shutting out the view. "There's been so many changes in this valley. People like it when things stay the same. It's been a lot to swallow, everything that's changed around here. Wears a person down, trying to keep up with it."

A group of middle-aged hikers in sun hats came out of the hotel and shoved packs into a Subaru. Headed for the Chalks, Lina guessed. She wondered if the Devils Staircase had been tamed with a switchback trail. Change came whether you wanted it or not.

"That first winter was pretty bad," Molly was saying. "A quarter of our town, destroyed. People had to live in camp trailers. You can imagine what that was like. No heat, no water. Many of them gave up. Sold out to city people for cheap. I wasn't sure any of us would make it. Ned, well, it broke him. You wouldn't know him, now."

A pack of river runners ran across the street with early morning beers. She and Molly turned to watch them. They were so young, the girls in bright river shorts, so unaware of what could lie ahead of them.

"But most of us did make it. And we're stronger for it. That's all Kelly is trying to say," Molly said. "But I just never understood you, that summer. You were my best friend. Well, until you weren't."

What could she say? Best friends had been such an important thing at fifteen. Hearts were broken so easily, small grievances nursed in silence and never forgotten. She had been thoughtless, unintentionally cruel.

Molly hoisted the baby higher on her hip, its hair as white as sugar. "We were kids, I guess. It doesn't matter now. You missed the big news, though. They finally identified Heartbreak Creek

Helen a couple of years ago. What are the odds that someone from Florida would show up here and know her?"

Heartbreak Creek Helen had loomed large in their lives. Girls were not safe in the world, they had concluded.

Her name was Lila, Molly said, and she was from way down in the swamps of the Florida Everglades. "She told her family that she wanted to see the world, and just disappeared off the map. Remember how we used to walk around in big packs? Nobody went anywhere alone. Well, except for Cassie. We all thought she was crazy anyway. Nobody would mess with her."

The child Molly carried squirmed in her arms, and she set him down on the sidewalk. He sat on his plump, diapered bottom and stared up at Lina with bottomless blue eyes.

"Tell me something, Lina. What was so special about Cassie? From everything I hear, she was one of those who used people up for whatever she wanted. I mean, if she had lived, chances are she'd be in some downriver shack barely making ends meet. You heard the stories about the Van Allens. People said she was a thief; she'd lift anything from your porch that wasn't nailed down."

Lina knew Cassie hadn't done all the bad things people assumed, but she hadn't been all good either. Maybe it was like that with everyone. Maybe Lina had been wrong all these years, assigning people to one category. Her father, a hopeless romantic in pursuit of a fictional treasure. Her mother, a victim of his desire. Rainy, too practical, giving up on dreams for stability. Herself even, permanently scarred on the inside, unlike Cassie's outward scars. Maybe she had poured herself into a mold that no longer fit her, a mold that was no longer true.

Before she could formulate an answer, a jacked-up Suburban

rolled up next to the sidewalk with a honk and a wave from a shaggy-haired driver. The metallic strains of Van Halen wafted from the open windows. "Oh gosh, that's Ben, I have to go," Molly said. There was an awkward pause as they faced each other. "Lina, it is so good to see you."

As she scooped up her baby and started to leave, Lina remembered something. She had forgotten all about the postcard.

"Did you write me a postcard?" she asked. "Was it you?"

"Postcard?" Molly shook her head. "I don't know what you're talking about. I didn't even know your address. I would have kept in touch but..." her voice trailed off. "Well, you know how it ended."

"Would Kelly or one of the others write me one? Pretend it was from Cassie?"

"From Cassie? No. Why would anyone do that? That's just insane. Kelly's mean, but she's not that mean. What's all this about a postcard?"

"Forget it, it's nothing," Lina said. She regretted saying anything to Molly. "I might ask Silas about it. I'm looking for him. That's why I'm here. Thank you for covering for me."

"Figured as much. Kelly and them didn't need to know that. Just start trouble, you know? People still talk bad about Silas Van Allen, but I think he's all right. You should get on up there and find him. He could use a friendly face. I think that man is about to die of plain loneliness."

Molly smiled and set her baby higher on her hip, yanked open the Suburban's passenger door and climbed in, facing forward, not looking back. She gunned it, scattering tourists in her wake.

Seven

The enclave of houses sprawled along a new and raw-looking road that snaked through the sagebrush just above town. They sprouted from bare lots, a few brave new saplings defying the elements. Each house was constructed of massive logs and boasted floor to ceiling windows facing the mountains. None of the windows had blinds, as if the owners knew that nobody would have the temerity to peek in. As Lina got out at a pullout by a cluster of mailboxes, she saw a concrete helipad at one of the houses, and an aboveground pool at another.

The houses were deserted, signs warning of dire consequences for trespassing posted by each driveway. Sprinklers hummed ineffectively against the heat, struggling to keep the new trees alive. It felt like a village of ghosts.

Lina was startled as a dusty forest-green pickup bounced toward her on oversize tires. It didn't belong in this neighborhood. Brakes needed to be replaced. Hoses too, maybe. The driver came to a halt next to her and a man stepped out. He lifted dark glasses off his angular face and narrowed his eyes. His voice did not sound friendly.

"Tazlina," he said. "Tazlina McCarthy. As I live and breathe.

Saw your father a couple days ago and wondered if you would be far behind. The hell you doin' here?"

It had been forever, fifteen years, a lifetime. But his voice still sounded the same: the rasp of sandpaper on reluctant wood. But older. No longer thirteen, now twenty-eight. A man, not the kid who had dogged her footsteps that last summer.

"Sort of in your face, aren't they?" he said, indicating the houses. "Hogging the view, like none of the rest of us want to see it. Those windows are a bitch to clean."

❖ ❖ ❖

She studied Silas. She would not have recognized him except for his eyes. Glacier blue, ice with ocean mixed in, just like Cassie's had been. Other than that, he looked nothing like the boy he had been. At thirteen, his jeans held up with rope, wheat-colored hair falling into his eyes, scrawny and hopeful, he had been almost hard to see. Back then, she had wanted to turn away from it. The way his bones seemed about ready to burst out of his skin, the way his whole body seemed hungry. He was all elbows and ears. Lina had once thought she could see his heart beating through his skin.

This man was someone completely different. His teeth were straight, hair cut short, and he had filled out his body. Okay, maybe he had grown only a few inches taller, just a head higher than she was.

"The trees have come back," Silas said. "But it still doesn't look the same. People remember. Some more than others. Like me. I don't forget."

Lina suddenly felt foolish, standing there in the imported gravel of a driveway that used to be a meadow. She thought of the postcard, hidden away in her backpack, but decided against pulling it out ... not yet. There was so much that she didn't know, but what had she expected? For Silas to welcome her back? For Cassie to appear with open arms? The last time she had seen Silas, he had closed a door on her, never wanting to see her again. She had thought the years might have softened him, but his expression was stone.

"Why are you here?" he repeated.

"I want to know what really happened," she said. "It's been haunting me all these years. That night ... why you wouldn't let me in, and what Cassie was doing up there on the mountain. Has it been haunting you the same?"

He didn't move, didn't uncross his arms. "Of course, it has. She was my sister. But what makes you think I want to open up all those scars again? There's only one thing I know about that night. You could have saved her, but you didn't."

"I tried to stop her, but it was so hot, Silas. You can't imagine how hot it was."

"I have, though. Maybe I wasn't there, but I've dreamed it a million times. So don't tell me I can't know what it was like."

"I loved her too," Lina said, an unexpected sob invading her voice.

Silas cleared his throat. He uncrossed his arms. "It's true there were things we didn't tell you. It was safer that way. But I don't know why it matters now. Knowing won't bring her back. It won't change what happened."

He opened the pickup door, a squeak of protesting hinges that needed some oil. Easy to fix, even easier to ignore.

"Listen," he said, "I'm glad you're all right. I did wonder about you. What they did to you. Nobody would tell me. But I can't go back there, I can't remember that time, I don't want to remember it, and it's not right of you to ask me."

She stood there watching him get ready to leave, silently scolding herself. This trip had been for nothing. She had left and crossed the canyon for no reason. It was time to give up, turn around, drive out of this slice of valley protected by impenetrable mountains and even more impenetrable people.

Lina was momentarily distracted by spray from one of the sprinklers catching the sun, turning the light into a rainbow of colors. One of the trees was dying, despite the water.

Her mind changed course, now remembering all the nights full of wind and regret. Without thinking it through, she stalked over and yanked open Silas' door before he could put the truck into gear.

"Listen yourself, Bullet. You're not shutting your door on me. Not this time."

A smile ghosted his lips. "Now that's a name I haven't heard in years." He swung himself out of the pickup. "All right, Tag. You got me. Old time's sake. You have five minutes to convince me."

Eight

Everyone in school called him Bullet but nobody remembered why. Lina's best friend Molly said it was because his father had always carried a pistol shoved in a holster on his jeans, a hunting rifle in a rack of the pickup. Maybe it was because the kid simmered like a shot ready to fire. Or maybe it was something else entirely. All Lina knew was he had a name, but nobody used it.

Bullet was not easy to like. His teeth stuck out like a beaver's. His long, pale hair hung in hunks around his shoulders and in his face. He was constantly pushing it out of the way, and it fell right back again. He wore the same clothes nearly every day—plaid flannel shirt, jeans so long he stumbled over them, a pair of Converse even in winter. He smelled like a stew of dirt and sweat and wood smoke.

But his eyes. They were a clear, unspoiled aquamarine, the color of a wild river. His eyes almost made up for the rest of him.

Bullet kept to himself, but it was no secret that he was the smartest student in the sixth grade. He was two grades behind Lina, but the school was so small—only a hundred kids—that everyone was known. Kids talked about him, for good reason.

He always sat in the back, as far back as he could get, whittling spoons out of lodgepole, a pile of shavings surrounding him.

The teachers talked about him too as they stood with their backs to the brick walls, enduring the brisk wind of recess. "Don't understand why he doesn't apply himself," Mrs. Finnegan said. "He understands the material. He's got one of those photographic memories ... it's kind of uncanny. But he doesn't even try."

"Says there's no money for college," Mr. Donegal said, and both teachers sighed. They were tired of talking to kids about scholarships, about pretending that everyone was equal, when everyone all knew it was a lie.

Even at fifteen, Lina knew that college was out of the question for kids like Bullet.

He hadn't had much luck to begin with. The family had been infamous for decades, living in a singlewide along Dabney Creek, cast-offs of their lives scattered through the sagebrush; cars that wouldn't run, refrigerators that had failed them. It was said that if you needed any part, any large appliance, that you could root around outside of the Van Allens' and surely find it. Whether it legally belonged to them was another story. It seemed like the family rotated in and out of prison, rehab and the mental hospital down in Boise, as though they were taking turns. His mama had vanished a few years back, his uncle was in prison from something nobody talked about, and his older sister, Cassie, had grown as wild as a feral kitten, spitting and fighting when forced to come to school until everyone just gave up. Why Bullet still came was anyone's guess. Maybe it was better than what he had at home.

If any trouble was stirred up in town, you could bet that a Van Allen was involved. The Van Allens were the lowest you could fall to; as long as there were Van Allens, you were doing pretty well in comparison.

Bullet was constantly being shoved and punched but didn't fight back. Instead, when tormentors approached, he faded into the distance. When they did catch him, he didn't seem to care, staring at them with those odd eyes. Although nothing had progressed beyond words and the occasional push, everyone at school could tell the situation was building. Soon, someone would step over the edge.

When Bullet was around, Lina wished he would just go away. Didn't he see how he was just making things worse? He seemed oblivious, sitting near the smoker's gate at recess, calmly whittling at a piece of wood. Why didn't he at least try to be normal? Maybe wear the same clothes as everyone else, talk to his classmates, stop the whittling. Everyone else learned long ago they had to fit in to survive. That meant jettisoning who they really were and becoming someone who was expected, who was familiar. That's why Lina wore the same clogs as every other girl, and skinny pants with zippers at the ankles. She curled her hair to fan outward and wore eyeshadow the color of the sky.

Being different was dangerous, and kids could sniff it out. Then they attacked.

The girls were more dangerous than the boys. Boys fought it out, and unless one of them was like Bullet, they subsided into a mutual understanding after the fists were done. You knew where you stood with boys. Not so with girls, who would stab you in the back as soon as you turned away. Lina had seen it, sheer meanness cloaked in words that dripped with false kindness. There was no part of a girl that could not be picked apart and found wanting.

The burnouts were the only people who seemed to accept Bullet. They occupied a particular rung on the social scale ... outcasts, but only because they wanted to be. They wore band T-shirts and carried boom boxes tuned to Nazareth. They hung out at the smoker's gate, even though not all of them smoked. In class, they slouched in the back row, expressions of disinterest on their faces. Everyone else was secretly a little afraid of them. Bullet wasn't part of their group, but they allowed him to exist in their orbit, as long as he stuck to the outer rings.

Bullet's sister Cassie was seventeen, her hair so blonde it was nearly white, corkscrewing wildly down her back without benefit of a comb. She rode a horse bareback down Main Street, a bottle in her hand, daring the cops or the truant officers to stop her. Sometimes she showed up in the Rod and Gun, throwing darts with such accuracy that nobody would play with her anymore. More often, she ghosted down a street, and after she passed by, people whispered that things went missing mysteriously, just old broken tools from their porches, or coolers missing lids, nothing anyone would really want. There were many rumors about her, but everyone knew to never say them to her face. Back in the eighth grade, Cassie had drop-kicked a girl down the stairs next to the biology lab for looking at her wrong. You didn't mess with Cassie Van Allen; everybody knew that.

But Cassie wasn't in school anymore, and Bullet was. He wasn't anything like his sister. He was colorless in comparison to the whirlwind that was Cassie. She had cast a shadow on everyone. Even though everyone pretended to look down on Cassie, Lina thought most of the girls envied her. They didn't know how to be strong, and Cassie did it with ease.

Bullet hardly ever spoke, although Lina knew he had plenty to say. She waited for him to say it, to stand up for himself, but he never did.

"Retard," the other kids called him.

❖ ❖ ❖

"Do you want to go to the woods?" Tony Ray asked as the party raged.

Lina shivered, even though the night wasn't cold enough to pretend that was why. She knew this question. It was the question girls both desired and feared. There was no right answer to this. Say yes, and you had the high beams of a boy's attention all focused on you, and wasn't that what you were supposed to want? But then you lived with the consequences: whispers circling around you as you walked the halls at school, being branded a skank.

But say no, and you were uptight, no fun, probably a lesbian, and relegated to a lower rung of the ladder. Even the other girls wondered why you thought you were too good for someone like Tony. The names were just as bad: Stuck-up. Lesbo, frigid.

She wasn't even sure if she liked Tony Ray, though she thought he was cute, and she didn't want to go to the woods with him. Going there seemed irrevocable, something she couldn't take back. Instead, she wanted romance, declarations of love, even a cheap heart-shaped necklace like some other girls wore proudly. Something other than the woods.

"Don't be scared," Tony Ray said, slinging a meaty arm around her shoulders. "We can just talk."

Lina hesitated, torn. Hadn't she wanted his attention? Why did it feel so treacherous?

"Come *on*," Tony Ray repeated. He tugged on her shirt, dragging her toward the line that separated light from dark, the lanterns from the unknown. "I didn't know you were such a tease." He pulled harder, making her stumble.

Lina made up her mind. "I don't want to. Leave me alone."

As they struggled in the wet grass, Lina realized something she should have known. Even though she had thought being a girl gave her power, men still held it all. There was the voice in her head suggesting she not make a scene. Go along with it or he might get mad. There was also the sickening futility of knowing that there was nothing she could do to stop what was about to happen.

The partiers were down by the river, oblivious. She could hear hoots of laughter as someone took a dive into the cold river. She could hear girls squealing as the boys tried to get them to take off their tops. Nobody would hear her over the music. Some of the guys might even think it was funny. They might even help Tony. She had seen boys come out of the woods, the girls silent, heads down, the high fives all around.

Suddenly someone was beside her, prying Tony's hand off her elbow. It was Bullet.

"Go back to the party and leave her alone."

Tony puffed up. He rolled his hands into fists. "What are you going to do about it, retard?" Tony again grabbed ahold of Lina's arm. "The lady's with me."

"Let her go."

"She's fine right here."

"I said, let her go."

"Make me."

Bullet's fist thrust out and Tony Ray dropped to the ground in slow motion. He lay still, his brown hair the same color as the old grass under the new growth.

"Let's get out of here."

"Is he breathing?"

Bullet rolled his eyes. "Of course, he's breathing. And he'll wake up pretty soon. Want to be here when he does?"

Lina wheeled and followed him up the hill to a lemon-colored Chevette parked with wheels off the pavement. Bullet cranked open the driver's side. "Get in this way, the passenger's is busted. Come on, unless you want me to leave you here?"

It seemed less dangerous, so she got in, plopping down next to him. Her feet straddled a crack in the floorboards where she could see pavement. She sat as small as she could on the slippery seat. If there was a seatbelt, she couldn't find it. Bullet gunned the accelerator.

"Should you be driving?" she asked. "Aren't you only thirteen? And can you please slow down?"

"Been driving since I was seven," Bullet said. He palmed the wheel carelessly, taking the curves on two wheels. "Got to put some distance between us and them. Unless you want to get out. Nothing between town and here, anyways."

She sat in uneasy silence, her hands clasped tightly in her lap, her eyes fixed on the river, lit up by the moon.

Finally, she asked, "why did you do that?"

He shrugged. "Didn't seem right, what he was doing. I was always taught to step in when someone needed help."

"I didn't need help," she said. "You didn't have to do it."

"Yeah. Okay."

"Wait. What are you doing out here at night, by yourself, at a party? Where are your parents?"

"I wasn't invited to the party. But I've never been to one. I wanted to go. I thought maybe if I stayed out of the way, nobody would see me. See how that turned out."

"Well, thanks. I guess."

"Cassie taught me that right hook," he said. "Pretty good, huh?"

"What's your real name anyway?"

"Silas. Bullet's just something kids call me in school."

Lina watched the featureless night whip by, the curves of the river. "Whose car is this?"

"My sister Cassie's. She found it in a junkyard and I got it running for her. Piece of crap mostly. Rear wheel drive. No good in snow."

"You got it running? By yourself?"

"Yeah. I like working on cars. I sell them, too, when I'm done."

Lina stared at Silas as he drove. She knew that she often thought of people as one dimensional, the face they presented to the world or what she had decided they were. Silas had always been Bullet, the kid everyone picked on. Now she saw him as someone who could take apart cars and put them back together.

"They're simple, cars are. Usually, it's easy to figure out what's wrong. They give you clues along the way. Like if the car stops running. Only a few things it could be, right? So I check the battery, or the alternator. Nine times out of ten it's one of those things. Unless you're a dummy and run out of gas. I have some mechanic books. I just tinker around until I figure it out."

He frowned. "Hear that? Engine's knocking. Probably the air and fuel mixture, or maybe the spark plugs aren't gapped right. Not too hard to fix."

They were coming into town now. A summer fog hung around, cooler air near the river trapped by the warmer layer above. Above that, the moon moved around the mountains. It was one of those perfect nights where she could understand why her parents had chosen this place.

"This is fine," she said, as they reached the foot of her road. They sat for a second in the darkness, the car humming in the silence.

"Aren't you afraid of what Tony Ray will do?"

"Nah," Silas said. "He's one of those guys who makes a lot of noise but doesn't back it up. Anyway, it's the last day of school. He'll be on the ranch carrying irrigation pipe all summer for his folks. He'll probably be gunning for you, though. Better stay out of his way this summer."

He hopped out of the car, and she slid over to the driver's side to climb out too. He was almost her height, barely five feet. The moon had dipped below the Isolations, to wherever it went, and his hair was so light it seemed to reflect the stars. Lina was overcome by mystery; there was so much more to Silas than she had ever known.

Who are you really, she wanted to ask. And how come I never knew this about you? But you didn't ask those things if you were a fifteen-year-old girl.

"See you around," Silas said. He got in the car, pushed it into gear and drove away. Lina stood there for a long time, watching his taillights, until they were swallowed up by the fog.

Rainy woke as Lina tiptoed up to the loft. She was late, later than she had ever been, but their mother was in her room with the door shut tight. Ever since their father had left, she had ceased to care where her children went. For once, she had declared the world was going to revolve around her. No more cooking, no more laundry that wasn't hers. If she felt like eating cereal for dinner, she was going to do that.

"Did she notice I wasn't here?" Lina asked in response to Rainy's unspoken question.

"Hello? It's our mother, remember? Unless we're bleeding out, she couldn't care less," Rainy said with a shrug. She switched on her bedside lamp, blinking in the explosion of light. "Was the party fun? Did Danny ever show?"

"It was kind of dead," Lina said. She slid under the covers. It felt strange, keeping this big of a secret from her sister, but Lina knew she wouldn't understand. To both of them, people like Bullet—Silas, she told herself—had always seemed contagious, like a virus. He could infect them and make them outcasts like he was. For survival, they had to keep their distance. There was no way Lina could tell her.

Nine

ilas was waiting for Lina to speak. She looked down the road, buying time. A red pickup was slowly negotiating the hairpin turns toward them. Far below, the town was small and insignificant, dwarfed by the mountains.

"Did you know where they sent me?" she asked. "Away from this valley, down to the desert. I haven't been back since."

"What was it like?"

"We called it the Bad Place. I lost everyone. Rainy. My family. You."

He nodded and leaned back, reaching into the cab to pull out a coffee cup. He pointed out over the rim of the road. "You know, this used to be my favorite place in the valley. I used to always stop here when I was hiking back up to the shop after school. I'd cut over from Nip and Tuck on a game trail when this used to be just grass and sage. This was the perfect place to see everything. The river, like a ribbon wrapped around the valley, the Chalks with the late afternoon glow on them like butter. It's not the same now, not with these houses in the way."

Their backs were to the Isolations, the forgotten mountain range, but Lina was still aware of them, their dark craggy cliffs and the afternoon shadow they cast. The Isolations never quite let you forget they were there.

❖ ❖ ❖

Silas seemed skittish, ready to bolt. She had to approach this the same way they had once tracked the wolves, their feet laid down carefully, heel to toe, barely remembering to breathe. She cast around for some way to reach him. He had loved those afternoons on the trails, just the three of them and the metallic clank of a shovel against rock.

"Do you still keep the ghost trails open?"

A slight smile. "No, after I got sent away, I don't think anyone ever went up there. Too many dead trees, all the brush, everyone still sticks to the Chalks."

"Have you been up there? To the Floor?"

"Plenty of other places to go," he answered. "Easier places." So, Silas really had changed, she thought. He had never been about easy.

"I've been back here a year," he said, opening up a little. "Four full seasons. Long enough to take the measure of the place. Long enough to know what's missing and what people haven't forgotten."

Lina understood.

"I forgot how cold it was here," he continued. "The air sinks into the valley at night and freezes the river, I swear to God. Was it this cold when I was a kid, because I don't remember that."

Silas, Lina recalled, had never worn a coat, even when the rest of the kids in her class had pulled the hoods of their sweatshirts deep over their heads, had swallowed themselves up in layers of wool and fleece. "Don't need one," he had said then when one of the teachers quizzed him about it. "Coats are for wimps." Now that Lina thought about it, she realized he had probably not had the money for a coat.

"They still talk about Cassie," he said. "They talk about her as if it was yesterday, not a dozen and more years ago. They probably got used to having nobody left to hate, and then I come along. It's made them all remember."

"Why go back then?" There were a million places in the world to go.

"I thought about not coming back, you know," Silas said. But he didn't have to say it: the valley was hard for leaving. Lina had not loved the place until she had met Cassie.

He grinned, fifteen years falling from his face. "The two of us, in the same place. Imagine the buzz in the valley."

Lina looked again where his eyes went. She had forgotten how this valley tugged at her heart. It was a place she couldn't sum up in mere words. From here, she could see where the Yellow River made a dogleg, water so clear she thought she could pick out rocks tumbling along the bottom. The mountains faced her, a row of jagged grey peaks dotted with permanent snow. Lina still knew all their names—God's Chair, Old Snowy, Starcatcher, and then the ones she couldn't see but knew were there, Miners, Wildhorse, Warbonnet. In all her years away she had not forgotten.

"I still feel like the same kid here sometimes," Silas said. "Like I never left. Scrambling all over these mountains in tennis shoes and a school backpack. But then I look up at these houses and I know time has gone by. Tell me, Lina. Why would someone own a place they hardly ever visited? When I go inside these houses, they even smell different, like loneliness would smell if it had a scent."

The way he was looking at her now made her believe they could be friends again.

"I treat it like a game sometimes," he continued. "I never see the owners, just the checks they leave me, but I try to piece together what they're like from the clues the houses give up. I swear to God, I can't help myself. I walk through the houses and look to see what I can find."

Pointing at random houses, he listed the discoveries. Dresses as ephemeral as mist hung from padded hangers in the first house; dozens of jars promising eternal youth lined the bathroom medicine cabinet. And over there, rows of pristine skis and snowboards were stacked in the mud room; a snowmobile sat untouched in the garage. And that house was packed with animal heads from all over the world, snarling down from the walls.

"At first, I felt like I was snooping," he said. "But now I consider it a necessity, like I have to gather evidence about these people who have invaded our valley. I poke through drawers, spin the locks of safes." He glanced at her. "I know what you're thinking. I don't take anything. Some of the old-timers would say that a Van Allen would steal as easily as breathing. Right? But I'm not that way."

"I know you aren't," Lina said, though she remembered Cassie returning from town with things she thought people would not miss. The hunt, the actual taking without being seen, was what she had desired.

The red pickup she had been watching gained the final hill and coasted to a stop next to them, the driver rolling down his window. An old truck, seventies maybe, but it ran smoothly, no knocking in the engine.

"Tony Ray," Silas scowled.

"Casing the joints, Van Allen?" Tony Ray blew a cloud of cigar smoke into the morning air, momentarily obscuring his face. His truck was immaculate ... except for a squat black gun on the seat next to him. Lina backed up a few steps.

"Just drinking coffee with an old friend," Silas said. "Contemplating the view."

Tony Ray turned his gaze, squinting in Lina's direction. Too vain to wear glasses, she thought. His hair was in a feathered style right out of the late seventies, although some of it was combed over to hide the encroaching baldness. He was no longer trim, the weight sitting heavily on his face and neck. The boy many girls had all loved from afar was long gone, buried under layers of fat and just plain mean.

"Well, I'll be damned," Tony Ray grumbled, staring at Lina with contempt. "Kelly was right, you did come back. I can't believe you had the guts."

"Come on, Tony," Silas interrupted. "Give it up. She's not here to cause trouble."

Tony Ray turned back to Silas, angrily stabbing his cigar out on the side of the pickup window, letting it fall to the ground. "All I know is here you are, the two of you together, again. Something's not smelling right. You up to something in the Isolations?"

"She won't be here long," Silas answered.

"Yeah? Well, you might have forgotten, but I haven't. Houses burned because of those two, Tazlina here and your sister. Including my house. Burned to the ground. The barn, the corrals, the livestock, everything. My mother was never the same after that. We had to declare bankruptcy. My dad had to go to work for Greenwood Ranch, a fifty-year-old man, working for someone else. And look who comes back here like nothing ever happened."

Silas assumed an expression of polite disinterest, but Lina could see his fist clench where he held his coffee cup. "I need to move along, Tony," he said. "Got work to do."

"Work," Tony Ray snapped. "Out of towners moving into the valley, driving up the cost of living, professing to be enchanted with the place and then setting about to change it to the place they came from. They want an airport, they want fern bars, they wanted a damn public swimming pool. Only thing worse are the locals who enable this crap ... people like you, Van Allen."

"We all do what we can to survive," Silas said.

"You keep telling yourself that. Meanwhile, I'd better not see either of you heading up to the Isolations. It's bone dry up there. Don't want a repeat of fifteen years ago. Go ahead, take a trip down memory lane and all that. Fix up your house, Tazlina, if that's what you're really doing. But both of you better stay out of the woods. I'll know if you go up there. I'll be watching."

"Seems to me that the Isolations are free," Silas said. "You don't own those mountains."

Tony Ray scowled. "Twenty-four hours, Tazlina McCarthy. Then you get out of my town. You'll be sorry if you don't."

He rolled up the window and drove back down the road, engulfing them in a cloud of dust.

Lina watched until the curves of the road hid the truck.

"Don't trust him," Silas said. "Can't put a finger on it, but he's shady. Always has been, even when we were kids. Did you see his pickup? Muddy well above the tires despite the dust. He's been driving up high, where there's still water. What's he doing up there?"

Lina furrowed her brow. "Someone downtown said the same thing ... 'we've all got a suspicion.' He hasn't changed one bit. Why do you think he's warning us off the Isolations?"

"Lina, Tony thinks he owns this whole place. Wants to be a bully. Always was, always will be."

The Isolations, she thought. Why not go there? Up there, she could breathe. Up there, maybe Silas would be happier, more like the boy he had been. Maybe she would be more like the girl she had been, too. The two of them, sweat running down their foreheads and soaking their shirts, free from what the world expected them to be.

"Tony's had a bone to pick for the last fifteen years," Silas added. "He's been cowboying over at Greenwood, but he would dearly love to get his dad's land back. Problem is some rich folk bought it up, built a new ranch, and have had it ever since. They're on the second generation now and Junior of the family has been talking about subdividing, building little ranchettes. Drives Tony crazy. From his bunkhouse at Greenwood, he can sit and watch the Range Rovers go in and out. Guess you're getting the picture."

Tony's pickup appeared at the base of the hill, navigating the final curves into town. Lina watched until it merged with the rest of the tourist traffic. "I feel like he's dangerous. Did you see the gun?"

"I did. But Tony's all bark, no bite. Been dancing around me ever since I came back. Trying to get me to throw a punch. Never has forgiven me for that one time down at the hot springs when we were kids. Hey. Forget him. It's almost lunchtime. I've got some time to kill. Want to go somewhere? Depressing as hell right here."

He turned in a circle, pointing at the jagged outline of the high peaks. "Lowest snowfall in decades, they're saying. Look at that, hardly any snow up there on Old Man. Rivers too low to raft. Forest Service is talking about shutting it down. I'll show you what happened to the hot springs. Get in."

Lina knew what her sister would say. Getting in a truck with a man she didn't know, a man who still held a grudge. Oh, Lina, Rainy would say, and roll her eyes. When will you ever get some sense?

But this was Silas, Lina thought. She had known him once. She saw him grin a little as he watched her make up her mind. Same old dance, he was probably thinking. One foot in, one foot out. That grin did it for her. She climbed in.

His pickup was patched together with whatever he had at hand: duct tape on the vinyl seats, rags stuffed in places where rust had eaten away the body. A starburst of cracks spread across the windshield. Inside, there were no clues to the man he was, just a thermos and a handful of plastic canteens that rattled around the cab. Some tools shifted in the pickup bed: shovels, pipe. Other than that, there was nothing to discover.

Driving down Nip and Tuck, they passed the ravine where a lost girl had haunted their lives.

"Remember Heartbreak Creek Helen?" Lina asked. "I heard they found out who she was."

"I heard something about that," Silas said. He palmed the wheel with one hand. "I also heard some talk that it was a Van Allen who had done it. Just like when anything bad happens in the valley. Things like that made me wonder why I came back. But dammit, I have just as much right to be here as anyone."

Lina thought of what Molly had said. *That man is about to die from plain loneliness.* Molly had been right. At first Silas had seemed hard as stone, but she was starting to see the cracks, same as the ones in the windshield she stared through. Eventually, if he did not take the time to fix it, the windshield would shatter, the weakness overcoming the strength that was once there. Unlike windshield glass, Silas' cracks would be harder to patch.

"Is it working, being here now?"

"I'm hopeful," he said. "Maybe in another twenty years the name won't mean anything anymore."

❖ ❖ ❖

It wasn't as far as Lina remembered to the pullout where the parties had always been. When she was fifteen, the drive had seemed dangerous and exciting, the headlights of the car bravely cutting through the darkness, the river a constant unseen presence beside them. Easy to be inattentive, to miss a turn in the road. There had been some close calls back then, boys in cowboy hats driving too fast, cars overturned. But now in daylight, it was only a few minutes downriver, a few mild curves on the two-lane road. Tame, really, not infused with danger after all.

"Hot springs is drowned now," Silas said, getting out. "The river changed and swallowed it up. Big flood a few years back. But we can still go down and sit there for a bit. Maybe someday the river will give it up again."

They walked down through the dry grass to the river's edge and sat with heels dangling over the place where the water used to be. The river had abandoned it and moved farther into the valley after carving out this exposed bank. Low enough to walk across without getting shoes wet, it had run out of steam. It seemed impossible that it had once been at flood stage.

"They took me to a place up by the Great Lakes," he said. "Heard of them? Freshwater lakes so big you can't see the other side. Lakes that make their own weather. I don't know why I went so far away except that most fosters don't want to take someone in as old as I was. Or maybe they wanted to get me away from any of my relatives, the ones still in prison. Not that they were in any shape to take me in, serving twenty to life. I stayed there until I was eighteen and I missed the mountains too much. So, I went up to Alaska. Worked the pipeline, got more money thrown at me than I ever thought I would see in my lifetime. Traveled some. Saw a few oceans. Decided to stick with land, not water. Almost got married a couple of times, but it didn't work out. I think my heart was always here. So, I gave in and came back."

"You didn't go on to college?"

"Oh, come on, Lina. I wasn't going to go to college. I wasn't ever going to be anyone special. The cards were stacked, and you know it."

"You were so smart. Smarter than any of us."

"Yeah, well, didn't get me very far, did it?"

In the end, only Rainy had found a normal life. She had never strayed from her plan: graduate from high school, go to college, get a well-paying job, marriage, kids. The rest of them had wandered off the map.

The river ran to their east, speaking like a third voice. Under where she sat, somewhere, hot water bubbled out of a fault line. The lines were hidden, but Lina knew they were there. Her father had shown them to her on the old geologic maps. These were the places where the earth breathed out, he had said. They were places where the raw and the tame met.

"Did you ever try to find me?"

"Not a chance," he said. "At first, I was just trying to survive without Cassie. In my new school it was different. Nobody called me any stupid nicknames. I played hockey, I played basketball, and on weekends I went ice fishing. Everyone told me this was a new start, a chance to be someone different. I believed them, because who wanted to be the way I was, one of the no-good Van Allens? If I looked for you and found you, I'd be right back there where I was. Then, it just seemed like so much time had gone by. I knew all of you were gone from the valley ... you could have been anywhere. And truth was, I blamed you. I guess I still do."

Lina nodded. She also still blamed herself.

"In that house," he said, and paused. "In that foster house, I always had enough food. It wasn't like here where Cassie and I had to decide what we could get from the store with what my father left us. Would we get cereal this time, or milk, because we couldn't have both. I had clothes too, clothes that didn't stink of transmission fluid or had belonged to somebody else, and water that didn't get turned on and off depending on whether he paid the bill. I didn't know people really could live like that, and I got used to it pretty quick. I didn't want to be reminded of the valley, or Cassie, or you either. I let myself forget for a long time.

"Then one night up in Anchorage, it was February, one of those nights when it's so far below zero that it doesn't really matter what temperature it is, I was sitting there waiting for word of when they'd need me back up on the slope. It was good money, you understand. Guys that hate it still go back, because of the money. You get sort of addicted to it. Anyway, I was in a buddy's house, sleeping on his couch, and he started talking about how he and his wife had once started to build a cabin back in the bush. They had canoed everything they owned up a river and picked out a spot and started to clear the trees around there. They were going to do it all by hand, cut down the trees, peel them, the works. 'But then what happened?' I asked him. 'Because I see you sitting here in a house in town drinking a beer with me.' He said that one night they were in their wall tent and they looked at each other and said that the wilderness was just too big for them to live out there all by themselves. What if he was on the snowmobile one day and broke through the ice and never got out? What if she met a bear by the garden? They hightailed it to civilization and never went back."

"The Floor," Lina said. "You remembered the Floor."

"God, yes, those stories we used to make up about that place. It hit me then, this longing to be back here. This valley, this river, the mountains, all of it. I think you can belong to a place, and if you ever leave it, you spend the rest of your life with a hole in your heart, wishing you could go back. So here I am."

He leaned back on his elbows. "Truth, Lina. I thought after I saw your dad that you might show up. I knew if he told you I was here that there was a chance of it. And honest to God, I'm not sure if I'm glad or mad or both. I've puzzled over it for years, what happened between you two. The last time you saw her. The last time anybody saw her."

"There's nothing more," Lina said quickly, automatically, even though there was. *A black coat, slipping through my fingers. Running down the mountain on our ghost trail, slipping and falling, a twinge in my ankle, but keep going, don't stop, harsh breath in my ears.*

Lina knew Silas could see her lie. She knew that she would have to tell him what had really happened, the night of matches and two girls and a forest ready to burn.

Ten

After the party at the hot springs, it occurred to Lina that she had rarely seen Silas outside of school, that he existed only there, that he had no other life. To her, he was just a kid, a fathomless two years between them. But he intrigued her, he and his sister Cassie. They didn't seem to care what others thought of them. They did what they wanted. They were free in a way she didn't know how to be.

❖ ❖ ❖

Rainy had been hanging around the house, waiting for the phone to ring. She lay with her feet up against the wall, snatching the cradle off the receiver to make sure it was still working. She wrapped herself in yards of coiled cord, willing Danny to dial their number.

"What a spazz," Lina said. She knew this would spark Rainy's temper, but she hated to see her sister mooning over someone. They had promised each other they would never do this, turn themselves inside out for a boy. They had said they would never give up the power that they thought they had at fifteen. Though Lina didn't quite understand it, she and Rainy knew how to use it. The sensual curve of an ankle, the casual bending of a neck; all those things translated into something Lina wasn't sure she could rein in, but that she knew she liked. It was only until the hot springs that she knew she had been wrong. Girls had no power.

"Stop it," Rainy said, hurt.

"*Stop it*," Lina mocked.

"Stop copying me!"

"Girls." Their mother wafted through the kitchen, smelling of coconut oil. She was coughing more then, discarded tissues in her wake like snowflakes. "I don't know why you can't just get along."

"She started it," Rainy said. She stomped up the loft stairs. Lina could hear the springs protest as she flung herself dramatically down on her bed.

"Tazlina. Go outside. It's a beautiful sunny day. Find something to do." Her mother rooted in the cupboard for a glass. "Can't imagine why I am coughing so much. Must be allergic to something." She flapped her hand at Lina. "Get out. Go."

She propelled herself out the door into a hazy afternoon, feeling mad at the world. It was early June, and the season was just getting started. If she had cared to look, the valley was bubbling with the promise of a summer as brief as the breeze. Tourists in brave shorts sported bulging backpacks and carried fly rods as they tried to push the season, the rivers still swollen with snowmelt. The shop owners who depended on a manic buying season that lasted only three months opened their doors and placed sale signs in their windows. Not yet beaten down by the constant flow of out-of-towners, they wore the big smiles of those who had made it through a long winter.

There wasn't anything for Lina in the river shop, the bar, or the pizza place. Molly had invited her downtown with the others, but ever since the party, Lina had felt a strange restlessness she could not explain. She had made a quick excuse, ignoring Molly's hurt silence. Now she wondered if she had made a mistake. Were the others talking about her? Had they seen her with Tony Ray? What were they saying?

She was about to go back home for lack of anything else to do when she spotted Silas, pushing his bike uphill. An ancient Huffy, it had two flat tires, but he kept at the task with resolve. He was heading up Nip and Tuck, the dead-end road that halted at the foot of the Isolations. Suddenly the day had a spark to it.

Keeping enough distance between them so he would not spot her, she began to follow him. The road snaked upward, making switchbacks into the slope. Soon she passed Heartbreak Creek where Helen had once lain, a place she wanted to avert her eyes from in case more dead girls lay there, pale arms entwined with the long summer sedges and cattails. As she passed the creek, Silas stopped at the place where the road widened, just above her. He stood there shading his face with his hand as if he were looking off into the Chalks for a reason. So that he would not see her, Lina ducked far down into the clammy weeds fringing the creek. Swampy, musty water seeped into her Chukka boots. Though she had never seen Helen's body here, she thought about how the girl had frozen into the creek that winter, her body turning to ice. The place seemed haunted. She was glad when Silas finally wheeled his bike around and she could leave.

The road ended with a flourish on a bench that had been once carved out by a bulldozer, as far as anyone could get with heavy machinery before facing a slope so steep that only a hiker or mountain climber could traverse it.

Silas headed for one of the shop buildings, one that was set off from the others, near the back end of the road. He dropped his bicycle on the ground and slipped inside a door on the side of the building. He didn't come back out.

Lina lingered for a minute behind one of the other buildings, sneaking glances at the one he had disappeared into. There were no identifying signs on it to tell her what it was. The other buildings clustered in a tight row along the road. One was a machine welding shop, long since abandoned; another, a failed self-storage. The wind picked up loose sheets of tin on the roof and banged them hard.

She waited, but nothing moved except the wind. Silas wasn't coming out anytime soon. Keeping to the side of the buildings, in case he could see out somehow, she headed back down Nip and Tuck. *What was he doing up there?*

Cassie was harder to track. Unlike her brother, who either didn't notice or didn't care who watched him, she stuck to the back streets. She darted across on the diagonals, lost Lina in the trees. She ran on her toes, leaving no footprints. Compared to her, Lina was clumsy, a bear to her fox. Silas was easier. He didn't look over his shoulder, not once.

Lina followed Silas twice more before she got caught. Both times he was on foot, once carrying a sack of groceries from the Merc, the other hauling two water jugs, one in each hand. Each time he opened the door just wide enough for his skinny body to slip through. There were no other clues. To solve the mystery, she knew she would have to get closer. Maybe there was a window around the back she could peer into.

She crawled through tall weeds laden with stickers on the

back side of the building. Burrs entwined themselves deep into her hair. Carcasses of dead cars were strewn back there, and their intestines: hoses, tanks filled with brown, thick liquid, hubcaps. Something fell over with a clatter, and she froze. No windows back here. Nowhere to hide either.

A hand shot out and grabbed her arm in a vise grip. She was face to face with the legendary Cassie Van Allen. Dragging Lina along, half off her feet, Cassie pulled her toward the door. "Look who I found," she said, giving a push that made Lina stumble and almost fall. "Nancy freaking Drew."

Lina struggled to get free, but Cassie's grip was too strong. "It's one of the twins," Cassie said. She kept her grip on Lina's wrist. "What do you want? Give me one good reason not to break your arm. I could do it, you know."

"Cassie," Silas said. He stood on the doorstep, blocking the entrance. "Back off. It's Lina. She's fine. She's not like the others."

Lina knew he was wrong; even though she hadn't been one of the ringleaders, she had stood by while Kelly and Susan had tossed fake love letters into his locker. While they had wrinkled their noses as he passed by in the hall. Something stinks. Ewww. Gross.

Cassie loosened her grip. "Whatever you say. But you can't come in here."

"Oh, let her in," Silas said. "We don't have anything to hide."

"Only because you say so," Cassie said. She dropped Lina's arm. "Up to you, Nancy. Stay or go?"

Lina gathered her courage and stepped inside.

❖ ❖ ❖

It was a cavernous room, lit by a row of overhead florescent lights. The floor was a hard, cold cement, banishing the warm June outside as if it had never existed. An ancient red Chevy pickup was disemboweled in the center of the room, tools scattered around it. A row of milk crates sat stacked against the far wall. There was one other door in the place, tightly shut. Bathroom?

"How come you keep following me?" Silas asked. He stood with hands on his hips.

Lina forced a brave tone. It wasn't Silas she feared; it was his sister, who stood too close, her eyes narrowed. "I'm not following you. Why would I be following you?"

"You are so following me. I've seen you a couple of times. Did Tony Ray send you up here to spy on me? You need to knock it off."

"Tony Ray didn't send me. Nobody sends me anywhere."

Cassie laughed, a short, sharp bark. Up close, she looked even more like a fox, with a chin so sharp it seemed it would cut anyone who touched it, and hair hanging like fur down her back.

"Where's your sidekick?" she asked. "I've seen you around town. The city twins, in their suede boots. Those satin jackets. Could tell right away you're not from here. What do you want with us, anyway?"

"Cass, stop," Silas said. "She's cool."

"If you say so," Cassie said. She sat on a lawn chair, folding her arms tight against her body. "But if you breathe a word of what you see up here, I'll thump you into tomorrow."

"I won't tell," Lina's voice wavered. "I just wanted to see what was up here."

"Then, don't just stand there," Silas said. "Check it out. I'm fixing up this truck. Doesn't run now, but it will."

"He's always under that truck," Cassie said, grudgingly deciding to accept Lina's presence. "It's the only thing our father left us. Silas thinks that if he makes it run, maybe it'll make Dad come back. Good luck with that."

"He comes back," Silas said. "He was just here a couple of weeks ago."

"To drop off a few bucks for his forgotten kids," Cassie muttered. "To keep the lights on in his precious shop and do whatever else he does. Noticed he didn't stay very long."

"Give it a rest, Cass," Silas said. "Lina, come here, I'll show you what I'm doing."

He pushed a padded cart with wheels underneath it toward her. "This is called a creeper. All the mechanics use them, so they can move around quicker, and they don't have to lie on the cold floor. You can slide under the chassis on this. Try it."

Lina inched herself gingerly onto the red plastic and used her feet to propel herself under the truck. Underneath, it felt like she was under some strange planet. Bulbous pipes hung just an inch from her head and mysterious fluids dripped onto the floor beneath.

Silas rolled in beside her. They lay together under the car on separate creepers. "Look, this is the guts," Silas said. "These hoses are the lungs, there's the stomach." He traced a greasy finger along the undercarriage. "That plate is what you'd take off to change the four-wheel drive fluid. It's not that hard, unless the bolts are rusted on. And see there? That round thing held up by what looks like baling wire? The muffler. If you don't have a muffler, the exhaust sounds like a gun firing. So, you want to have a muffler."

"How do you know all of this stuff?"

"Simple," he said. "All you need to do is follow the lines. Everything under here connects to something else. It's all related. If one thing doesn't work, then the next thing doesn't, and pretty soon the truck won't run at all."

"Boring," Cassie said from somewhere above. "Let's do something else."

"Let's go to the trails then," Silas said. He rolled out from under the truck in one quick motion, leaving Lina alone. She didn't like being under there by herself, as if the weight of the metal above her would crush her flat. She rolled out too.

Cassie was out of her seat like a shot fired. "Don't tell her about the trails."

Lina's curiosity overcame her fear of Cassie. "What trails?"

"Now you've done it." She paced, her eyes flashing. "We don't tell anyone about the trails."

"Cassie. Once in a while, you've got to trust people. Tell her or not, I don't care." Silas shook his head and disappeared under the truck again, the only sign of him his muddy sneakers.

Lina rolled back underneath too. She could see Cassie's clunky brown hiking boots as she moved around the room. It felt safer to be under the car with Silas.

"It started because we were following our dad," he said. "Cassie won't tell you this, but I will. Don't worry. She'll get over it. Won't you, Cass?"

Silence.

"We have a set of trails," he said. "I mean, they aren't real trails, but then again, they sort of are. The thing is, they're both real and not real."

"If you're going to tell her, do it right," Cassie said. "Come out from under there, both of you. Hiding under there like a pair of rabbits."

Sheepishly Lina rolled out and sat up on the creeper. Cassie squatted down next to her. "This isn't a game, City Twin," she said. "If we tell you, you have to swear to secrecy."

"I will," Lina said, feeling a flash of excitement. This was something different, something new.

"Okay, but you breathe a word of this and you're toast." She was so close that Lina could smell her breath—a strange combination of coffee and mint.

"I won't," Lina whispered.

"We're building trails," she said. "We hike up in the mountains with our tools and we clear trails."

Lina felt the sting of disappointment. *Trails?* She didn't care about trails. "That's your big secret?"

Cassie scowled. "Yes, trails. We only work on the old trails. The ones the rest of the world has forgotten about. We call them ghost trails. Trails that the miners or the sheepherders used to use. You can still find pieces of them, a blaze on a tree or the hint of tread. I love trying to find those trails. We find them and bring them back to life. It's like solving a mystery."

"We have trails all over these mountains," Silas boasted. "Trails nobody knows about but us."

When she spoke, Cassie's face was transformed, became almost beautiful. "It's like a mission," she said. "We don't want them to be forgotten."

"Why would anyone care if you did that?"

"Trust me, people would care. People always care when you try to do something good. They'd come up with all sorts of reasons why we shouldn't do it. It's probably illegal, since it's not our land, it's Forest Service. It's wilderness. We might be disturbing some plant. Making a highway for wolves to get down to town. I don't know. But just keep your mouth zipped

108 - The Lightning Within Us

or I'll make you wish you hadn't."

Lina had no special love for trails, but she watched Cassie with fascination. She was convinced that she wanted some of what Cassie and Silas had, the type of confidence that allowed them to make noise in the world, instead of creeping through it like a mouse. None of the girls at school had what they had. If she stayed with them for a little while, maybe it would rub off on her.

"Can I come with you?"

They exchanged a glance.

"We've never taken anyone before," Silas said.

"I know, let's take her up the Devils Staircase." Cassie smiled and turned to Lina. "If you can handle that without crying, you're in."

Lina knew about the Devils Staircase. It was in the Chalks, off trail. Kids dared each other to climb it but nobody ever did. The risk was too great. Boulders the size of Volkswagen Bugs littered a steep chute between two rock outcrops. Between them, sliding fields of smaller talus, the kind that could break an ankle. A fall would leave you sliding inexorably to waiting rocks below. Two hikers had died in the Staircase that summer, one plummeting in an oversized cartwheel just shy of safety, the other slowly perishing alone with a broken femur.

The reason people tried to take the Staircase was that it was a short cut to an alpine basin on the other side. Hikers were all about short cuts. The other way to get there was a long slog through a tedious forest with no views, a green tunnel that wasn't the reason why people came to the Chalks. They only had two days off, a week at most, and they wanted to spend it up high, at the lakes. The long way was a fifteen-mile trek uphill in a parched landscape, hauling as much water as you could stand. The Staircase was a tempting alternative, even though the rangers tried to talk people out of it as much as they could.

"Don't know," Silas said. "That's not a beginner climb."

"I'm not a beginner. I've been in the Chalks."

It was true; their mother had herded Lina and Rainy along to some of the lakes the September they had moved to the valley. They had to see them, she insisted; seven months of winter was coming, and all too soon the lakes would be inaccessible. Lina had trudged along behind her mother's power walk, unable to understand what was so intriguing. The lakes had been beautiful though, sheets of blue in the white granite for which the mountain range had been named. Their mother had chattered endlessly about spirit places and healing, and how the girls should be intentional in every action. "Can we go now?" Rainy asked. Their mother had gotten mad and marched double-time back to the car, refusing to speak to them for the rest of the afternoon.

"The Chalks," Silas said. He rolled his eyes. "My great grandmother hiked the Chalks in her seventies."

"I can do it," Lina insisted, though she was far from sure.

"Your funeral," Silas retorted. "We have to take the car, we can't walk from here. So you have to ride with us."

Cassie looked her over. "Are those the only shoes you have? Have you ever hiked in your life? Where's your boots?"

"I don't have any boots. Just these Chukkas." They were city shoes, Lina saw, looking at the sturdy leather boots that Cassie wore. In the city, these had been what the popular girls wore, brushed tan suede and rubber soled. City girls wouldn't be caught dead in Cassie's boots.

"They'll have to do. You don't need a water bottle, we drink

from the streams. We'll get you a backpack if you come back."
They slid three across into the same Chevette she had ridden
in before. "Back seat's torn out," Silas said. "Since I'm the
youngest, I'll straddle the gearshift."

The sour tangy odor of their bodies filled the car. It wasn't
unpleasant, just different from the way normal kids smelled,
the girls cocooned in Avon and Loves Baby Soft, the boys
optimistically sporting Old Spice. Cassie and Silas smelled
real, the way everyone probably smelled underneath the layers
of perfume and deodorant they wore.

"Do you even have a license?" Lina asked.

Cassie snorted. "Do you have a license?" she mocked. "What
do you think? I know how to drive. Unless you want me to let
you out right now."

Lina closed her mouth, thinking of her house, Rainy with the
phone cord stretched as far as it could go away from Lina,
their mother lying on a towel in the front yard. She didn't want
to go back there. They passed through town at a sedate, non-
attention-attracting pace, and Cassie sped up as she took the
right onto the state highway. She cracked the window and lit
up a joint, one hand on the wheel. "Don't tell me you've never
smoked either."

"I tried it," Lina said, "in the city. "Didn't like it, really."
Smoking reminded her too much of her father, the way he lit
one cigarette with the butt end of the other while he studied
maps.

"Sometimes my heart races," Cassie said. "It's the only thing
that calms me down," Cassie said. "Don't even ask, Silas. You're
a baby, much too young for this."

Five miles from town Cassie turned sharply onto an unpaved
forest road, the tires skittering on washboard. The farther they

went, the more Lina felt as though she were heading into a new life. This felt big and mysterious, as if she could be a different girl entirely, free from the hierarchy of school, the constant vigilance of presenting herself to the world in one prescribed way.

The trailhead was packed with out-of-state vehicles and a couple of rusty horse trailers. Even though it was June, the trails barely melted out, a steady line of hikers climbed like ants on the first switchbacks, bound for the high country. "We have to take the tourist trail for a few miles," Cassie said. "Necessary evil. But we don't have time for a lot of questions. Where are your parents, how much farther to the lake, do you have any water? Just keep walking, no matter what."

She was right; people littered the trail like causalities from a war. They perched on logs, feet bare, plastering moleskin on newly sprouted blisters. They slumped beside their overstuffed backpacks, likely regretting every single luxury item that they had brought. Few looked up or spoke. Lina thought that she saw admiration in the eyes of those who did, as the three teenagers walked swiftly up the trail, each with an easy stride.

Or at least, Silas and Cassie seemed to belong in the wilderness. Back in town they hadn't looked quite clean. Their cheeks were smudged with dirt, and Lina had noticed that when Cassie shook her hair, wood chips fell out like a rain shower. Silas' jeans were pocked with holes and his socks were permanently gray. But out here, they turned into different creatures, their skin the color of brown sugar, their bodies moving more like small, swift animals than people as they steadily climbed up the pass that separated one set of rivers from another.

The trail stretched itself out lazily along an open ridge, lined with bright yellow flowers her father had called arrowleaf balsamroot, the first tentative flowers to show their faces before all the others followed suit. Her feet crunched on sharp pieces of shale, a warm summer wind blowing her hair.

The basin they walked through was tipped toward the sky like a hand curled upward, fresh new grass a spiky carpet. Tiny lakes reflected the harmless clouds overhead. A few dome tents perched on the edges of the lakes, and Lina saw a man fishing on a rocky point, drops of water catching the sun as he cast back and forth. Cassie pointed. "Just up ahead, that's the Staircase."

Did people really climb that slope? It didn't look so bad at first, stair stepping in a series of ledges to the place where the real climbing would begin. "Don't walk single file here," Cassie said as they left the main trail. "If we all walk in a line here, we'll pound out a new trail."

"What's wrong with that?" Lina asked. She stood trying to catch her breath. Up here, a thousand feet higher than the valley, the air was elusive, and forcing it down her lungs was harder than she had anticipated.

"Don't you know anything?" Silas said. "It's called leave no trace. When you go cross country, you're supposed to spread out. If we don't, our feet will make a trail. There's places where trails aren't supposed to be. Like this." He indicated the soft, vulnerable grass under their feet. "So just do what she says."

Lina walked parallel to Silas; Cassie having grown impatient with their pace. "What about your dad?" Lina asked through shallow breaths, hoping to distract herself as they headed upward. "What were you following him for? Where was he going?"

"We didn't know at first. He started out in the Chalks. He

would come in to town and give us some money, enough to last for a couple of weeks. Don't tell anyone I'm not still living here, he'd say. He said that if anyone knew, they'd pack us off to juvenile hall. Then he'd grab a backpack and a cold chisel—do you know what that is? Never mind, not important. He'd head up into the woods and cut off of the tourist trail and when he came back down, right before he left, the pack would be full. We wanted to know what he was doing. We had a car that would barely run, but we would get in it and follow him to whatever trailhead he went to."

"What was it? What was he doing?" Her breath was ragged in her ears as she tried to keep up. Cassie was a blur in the distance. She balanced on a rock far ahead. "Come on, you snails," she called before jumping down.

"Crystals," Silas said. "Have you ever seen them?"

"No. What are they?"

"Seriously? Haven't you ever been in the mountains?"

"Not really. Just to the tourist trails."

He paused and regarded her curiously. "How come?"

"I just don't really like the outdoors."

"How can you not like the outdoors?" Silas looked puzzled.

Lina cast about for reasons. "I don't know. Bugs. Wild animals. And it's scary. You can get lost."

"Oh boy, you've got a lot to learn."

Lina hurried to keep up, disregarding the clatter of stones sliding under her boots. "What about the crystals? What are they?"

Silas' face lit up. "They're the coolest things ever. All the colors of the rainbow—smoky quartz, yellow topaz and my favorite, the ones the color of lakes. They're hidden in granite in cracks and holes. You have to hunt for them. If they're open to the sun they fade and lose their color."

"But how do they get there?"

"Don't know exactly," Silas said. "I read a book where it said that some come from when magma cools, but I don't believe it. I think they come from God."

Lina thought of her father and how he denounced God. She decided to let that go for now. "But why do people take them?"

"People chisel them out of the rocks and sell them. Collectors will pay big bucks for a good crystal. Like, hundreds of dollars. I don't really know why because they don't do anything. They just sit there. But I guess people like to look at them. People like to own pretty things."

"Isn't that illegal?"

"Duh, of course it is. It's the wilderness. You aren't supposed to take anything out of the wilderness."

"So, did you tell on him?"

"Are you crazy? He'd go to jail. And as soon as they found out we weren't living with any adults, we'd go to juvie."

"But..." Lina stopped walking and stared at him. "You're as bad as he is if you don't tell."

"What world do you live in, Lina? We have to look out for ourselves. And don't tell Cassie I told you. She'd have a cow. Come on, we're almost there. This is the worst part."

What? She took a shallow breath.

The two of them stood at the base of the chute, looking upward. "See that notch?" Silas asked, pointing. "That's what you aim for. Doesn't matter how you go."

"Where's the trail?" Lina asked.

Silas laughed. "There isn't a trail. That goat trail to the left, maybe. But it peters out not too far from the top and you might get cliffed out. Better just pick a way and go."

Standing there, the route looked impossible to her. The throat of the chute was littered with rocks jagged as teeth. It was as if a giant had thrown a tantrum and sent boulders tumbling down the mountain, leaving them where they lay.

"This is where the tourists usually turn around," Silas said. "We call it Chicken Out Point." He grinned. "Don't tell me you're one of them."

"I'm not," Lina said. She wasn't sure if she was telling the truth. Silas climbed above her, his body seemingly held together with pieces of flexible rope. He ascended the boulder field with leaps and jumps of faith, landing on one foot, showing off. "It's not that hard, honest," he called as she began to pick her way through the jumble of rocks.

The chute had slimmed into a narrow throat, with steep rock walls on either side. The terrain had steepened, with what felt like a sea of loose rock cascading in waves every time she moved. Silas was perched above her, squatting on an outcrop. "Here, just sidestep over to this ledge," he said. "Easy peasy. Just jump."

Lina froze in place, her legs refusing to obey. The gap between where she needed to go and where she was yawned before her, impossible. If she fell here, her body would tumble in a freefall all the way to the bottom. Her eyes pricked with hot tears. "I can't."

"Sure you can." Silas scrambled down with ease and demonstrated. "Put one foot there, on that rock. It won't move, I tested it. Then swing your other leg around to this one. You got it."

"Don't be such a chicken," Cassie hollered from somewhere unseen above.

Lina knew she would never be like Silas and Cassie. She

didn't belong here at all. What was she trying to prove? She clung to a rock taller than she was, its grainy surface still cool from the night, the sun somewhere far away, too far to bother with her.

"Told you she would quit," Cassie said. She had climbed down from the top and was perched on a rock the size of a dinner table just above Silas.

"Yep, she just can't do it," Silas agreed.

Lina glared up at them and blew the hair out of her face. She hated the way they must see her, red-cheeked and miserable. "I'm not going to quit," she muttered through clenched teeth. She would show them. Tentatively she stretched her left foot toward the rock Silas had indicated. A clatter of pebbles erupted underneath, bouncing and sliding their way down the mountain. She swallowed hard and leapt, her feet landing solidly on the ledge.

From there it was only a short scramble to the top, hand over hand. She pulled herself up, one knee scraped and bleeding, to stand next to the others.

"You did it!" Silas said. "Knew you could. High five!"

"I didn't think you could," Cassie said. "Thought you'd give up halfway and we'd have to carry your butt down. Guess you're tougher than you look."

They stood on a small slice of ridge, only wide enough for the three of them. To the south, chalk-white peaks spiked a moody sky. To the north, the safer tourist trails spread out, a thousand feet lower than they were. Below them, a slate-colored lake was ruffled by a breeze Lina could not feel, surrounded by a rocky basin.

Cassie spread her arms out wide. "We're on top of the world, Tagalong! How does it feel?"

Her legs unable to hold her, Lina sank down to sit on a low carpet of spiky plants bearing white flowers.

"Check it out," Silas said, squatting next to her. "Look at how neat the flowers are, like little bells."

She peered closer. He was right. Until she looked, really paid attention, she would have completely missed the flowers, lost in the green mat of the plant. "What's it called?"

"Don't know. Cassie and me, we make up names for all the flowers we see out here. This one we call winter's breath, on account of this ridge only being free of snow a few weeks a year. It's almost always winter up here."

"I can feel it coming," Cassie said from where she stood, toes on the edge of the ridge. It was only June, but she was right. Up this high, the air was too thin to hold much warmth. Patches of old snow lay just below the ridge, the sun unable to gather enough strength to melt them.

"Hey Tag," Cassie said. "If you could have a superpower, what would it be?" Without waiting for an answer, she said, "I'd be able to fly. Sometimes I pretend I can. I stand like this on the edge of the ridge and lean against the wind, like this."

"Cassie, get back," Lina shouted, as if suddenly they were best friends. "You'll fall."

Cassie laughed, staggering a little as she regained her balance. "Well, Tag, you didn't answer my question. What's your superpower?"

"Why are you calling me that?"

"Because, you're tagging after us like a little puppy. So, your superpower? What would it be?"

"I don't know." Lina shredded the stem of a winter's breath in her fingers. "Maybe read minds?"

"Ugh, why?" Cassie sat cross-legged next to her. "Like you'd even want to know what most people were thinking."

"I'd be invisible," Silas said. "Just think of how I could mess with the kids at school. Turn over their lunch trays, trip them on the playground. It would be so cool."

"Flying's the best," Cassie said, and Lina had to agree. "When I was a little kid," Cassie went on, "I used to think I could fly. I mean, don't all little kids think that? But I really, really did think that. I thought if you leaned against the wind, and you really believed, it would work. It never did. But when I grew up, I realized that you could fly in your mind. If something was going on that you didn't want to be a part of, you could just close your eyes and fly away."

Cassie jumped to her feet. "What are we doing sitting up here all day? Let's go back down."

"Cassie?"

"What now, Tagalong?"

"Did you mean that, about thinking you could fly? Did you ever try it?"

"I told you. I was a little kid. Little kids believe all kinds of things that aren't true."

Lina looked down the Staircase, gathering her courage. Going down looked equally as hard as going up. Cassie had already begun her descent, rocks rolling with abandon as she galloped down.

"Let's go," Silas said, nudging Lina's arm. "I didn't finish telling you about the trails."

As they made their way downward, he chattered on as if he had not had an audience for years. Maybe he hadn't. "So anyway, like I said, our dad stuck to the Chalks. Easier walking there. But then the Chalks got popular. They got written up in the paper when it became a wilderness, and more and more people showed up. We figured he was worried he'd get caught there. That's when he moved to the Isolations. One day we were following him and found one of these old trails. Those were more interesting to us than whatever he was doing."

"Did you ever catch him?"

"No. He was sneaky. I think he knew we were following him. He ditched us every time. We'd find where he had been, the holes where the crystals used to be, empty pockets in the rock. The thing is, we never figured out how he pulled it off by himself. The crystals are easy getting, but you have to take them to Boise or some other big city to sell them. How was he doing it? We never guessed, and of course he never told us."

"Is he still hunting crystals?"

"He gave it up, I think. At least, he never sticks around long enough to go up there. The Isolations are tough. Nobody goes up there. Nobody but us."

He leapt to a lower rock. "Come on, going down is fun. You can ski it. Watch." He flung himself down the scree, sliding on his boots, making giant steps as he went.

"Go bigger," he called, turning around. "Not those little hops. What are you, a bunny?"

Lina laughed, a bright, happy sound she hadn't remembered making in a long time. She gave herself to the mountain then, half running, half falling. As she made huge, jumping leaps, she felt as if she were flying.

Eleven

"That summer felt like magic," Lina said. "Remember?"

"Of course, I remember," Silas said. He glanced at his watch. "It's getting late. Maybe I should bring you back now. Maybe it's better if we just leave it like this."

But he didn't move. Lina watched a water ouzel dip in and out of the river, looking for bugs. The water was low, so low she thought that she could walk its entire length, down through the canyon to the Snake and beyond that to the sea.

"Are you worried about Tony Ray?" Lina said. "Because it's me he's after. Not you."

Silas took a flat stone and whipped it out over the river. Lina remembered him doing this when they were young, always skipping rocks. He had tried to teach her how, but no matter how hard she tried, her rock had always thudded in the river without grace. This time Silas' rock skipped once, twice, three times before plopping into the water. Rings spread out where it had been, and then it was gone.

"The last time I saw you," Silas began.

"I was fifteen," Lina countered. "You know what it was like then. You know what school was like. All those rules that weren't written down."

From somewhere beyond where she could see, a coyote howled. It was joined by several others, distant yips and barks cascading down the scale until they finally went silent.

"The wolves," Lina said. She knew she was buying time, but Silas wasn't moving either. "Tell me about the wolves."

Silas took a stick and drew circles in the hard dirt near his feet. "Don't know much. Fish and Game collared a few. Some of them got in trouble, went after the sheep up in Sixmile Creek. People are saying these are a different type of wolf, the ones they brought into Yellowstone from Canada. More aggressive, meaner. Don't know much about that. But word around town is that there's less wolves now than there were. That they are disappearing."

In the mountains, she thought, you could fool yourself into just about anything. A bear instead of a dark stump. An easy ford instead of a creek that tugged you off your feet. A lake that you could swear you were the first to see, planted there just for you to find. Maybe this was the same. Maybe the wolves had never been there at all. But she knew that was wrong.

"We heard them," Lina said. "Remember? They were here."

"I know it." He looked out across the expanse of trees across the river as if they would give up their secrets. "From what I hear, the wolves divided this town. Some of the wolves came into the allotments, killed sheep, killed cattle. People lost friends over it. Families split up. It wasn't a good time for a while. Things seem to have evened out now. The wolves haven't come down from the high country in a long time."

Lina wondered if the wolves were hiding up there somewhere, biding their time, waiting for everyone to forget they were there. Maybe they had decided that there were safer places to live.

The wolves were never supposed to be here in the first place, but they were. They had crept south and west like a slow tide, filling in the gaps that had been left when their ancestors were poisoned, shot, hunted out decades before.

"Silas, remember the time we heard them? We were up at the Floor."

"Cassie howled back," he answered, his face inscrutable. "You were so scared."

"I thought she was going to call them in to us."

"She loved wolves," Silas said, "or the idea of them anyway. She never let me tell anyone that we heard them. They would have been collared, trapped, every move they made watched. 'Nothing should live that way,' she said."

Lina remembered the three of them walking through the night, the light from their torches one long line. Cassie had talked the whole way down the trail, telling them that people were scared to death of wolves. That the only people with the right to gripe were the ranchers, who didn't need one more thing to tip them over. Still, Cassie had said the wolves were here long before any of us were. It isn't our right to kill them.

"Ah, the hell with it," Silas said. His voice was rough. "No more memory lane. You should get on the road. It's a long drive, it'll be close to midnight when you cross the Snake."

They walked up to the pickup, Lina trying to figure out what to do next. Tony Ray's threat bothered her more than she thought it should. It wasn't like she was going to start another forest fire. Was it just plain anger that fueled him? Or was it something else?

On the highway, a rancher with a hay truck coming the other direction lifted a finger off the wheel the way people did around here, whether you knew them or not.

Lina remembered the hostility on the faces of her former friends. "How do they treat you?" she asked. "Kelly and Jim and the rest." She told him how frightened she had been at first, surrounded by the crowd next to her pickup.

"They look right through me," Silas said. "Like I'm invisible. Won't talk to me unless they have to. I go days without speaking."

"How do you stand it?"

"Get used to it after a while. Maybe it'll change one day."

Lina couldn't imagine facing stony expressions every time she walked down the road. But then she remembered Joe Grider telling her that she locked herself away on Starvation Road, refusing to go to potlucks or dances, not even giving folks a friendly smile.

"Think I'll drive up the south fork of the Yellow to the end of the road," Silas said thoughtfully. "Listen for the elk bugling in the aspens. Spend some time on my own."

He didn't ask her to come along.

As the truck labored up Nick and Tuck, they sat in uneasy silence. Lina twisted her hands in her lap, trying to find the right words to say. The hostility of the locals, Tony Ray's menacing words, and now Silas, switching back and forth from warm to cold, all contributed a stew of unease that churned in her belly. Had she gone too far with the memories of Cassie, dredged up secrets that Silas wanted to forget?

"I've studied what fire does," Silas said. "Manzanita comes back first. That is, if there's enough seeds and rain in spring. In places, the fire burned right down to the bedrock. Nothing can come back from that. But if there's a way to survive, the lodgepoles know how to do it. That's what happened here. Eventually the trees shaded out the brush. My dad used to call it doghair, the trees grow so thick at first. Then they thin out. The best ones make it. The others don't."

Back up at the empty houses, nothing had changed. The same wind moaned around the outbuildings and tossed the leaves of the new, young trees. "Here it's already fall," Silas said, "And some of these people haven't been here all summer. Makes you wonder." He stuck out his hand. "Be safe. Live a good life."

Lina watched a small plane buzz the dirt airstrip south of town. Tourists, maybe, back from a float trip in the Salmon Breaks. She didn't want to leave, not now, when she felt so close to solving the last piece of the puzzle. She knew it would be the last chance she had, her last tie to Cassie, the last opportunity to lay it all at rest. *You've got twenty-four hours*, she thought, and shivered. Despite Silas' assessment of Tony Ray, she had seen his eyes. She knew he meant it.

And there was Silas. She had caught glimpses of a raw scar inside of him, something that she could possibly help heal. She found herself caring about Silas, the kid he had been, the man he was now, with a haunted look in his eyes that she thought must match hers. How could she leave now?

"I have an idea," she said. "I think we should go up there, to the Floor. Silas, hear me out. It seems like we both want something. You want to know what Cassie told me that night. I want to know what secret you both were keeping, what made her go up there in the first place. Let's both go up there. Let's find the old trail and pack in our bedrolls and spend the night. We'll tell each other everything. No holding back."

Every scenario she had imagined about being back in the valley didn't include going into the Isolations. She almost wanted to take it back. Once the Isolations had been the best and worst place she had ever been.

"Are you sure that's what you want?"

Suddenly going to the Floor seemed like the most important thing in the world. If they could put the past to rest, that would be the place. Lina closed her eyes and took a chance. No more poker face, just this one time. When she opened her eyes, she said, "You wanted to know how I was. I'm afraid, Silas, afraid of everything. I need to stop being afraid. The only way I can do it is to go up there. Go to the Floor, where it all began."

Silas took his time. He stared out over the valley, his eyebrows knit in thought, or maybe pain, she wasn't sure which. "And where it ended," he said.

"Silas. Please. I can tell you don't think much of me anymore, but can we do this? For us? For Cassie?"

He turned away from her, his voice breaking. "Haven't you done enough?"

She felt as if she could not stand, as if her body would not hold her upright. "I can't sleep," she said, forcing the words out. "I lie there at night and listen to the wind coming off the Wallowas like a freight train, and it all comes back. I can't live like that anymore. Can you?"

He whirled to face her. "I'd give anything to sleep through the night. Instead, I see her face. I hear her laughing, the way she used to on the trails when we were too slow to keep up. I can't make her go away."

A chill ran through her, deep as winter. "Me either," she whispered. "So, what do we do? How do we make it stop?"

"We go," Silas said. He slapped his hand on the truck hood. "We go to the Floor. You and me. You're right. It's time to go back. It's long past time to go back."

Twelve

Lina had noticed that Cassie always wore the same thing: a long-sleeved plaid button-down and a ragged skirt that hung below her knees. Her only concession to cold was a black coat, several sizes too big for her.

When they had walked up to the Devils Staircase, Lina had seen how Cassie hiked up her skirt, tucking the tail in her waistband, her skin so dark from trail dust that Lina couldn't tell her true color. Silas had whispered to her then that Cassie didn't have other clothes, not really. Well, she did, he amended, she could wear the clothes their mother had left behind, but one day Cassie had hauled most of them into the gravel and lit a big bonfire. She had only kept the things that might be useful someday: a pair of broken-down hiking boots, flowered shorts and a tube top for when she washed the others. There wasn't any money for new clothes. Their father left them just enough to eat. Cassie didn't care about clothes anyway, he said. They just got dirty, and you had to wash them.

The day after they climbed the Devils Staircase, Lina stole into her father's closet. He had kept his clothes separate from her mother's, as if what he wore was not to be mingled with anyone else's belongings. She pulled some of his shirts to her nose; the same crushed grass smell of him still clung to the fabric.

She went into her mother's closet too. Stuffed in the back were relics of the woman she had been: river skirts, gauzy and transparent, halter tops that tied behind the neck. She would never wear them again. They would never be missed.

❖ ❖ ❖

"What's all this stuff?" Cassie said, emptying the paper bag while glaring at Lina. The contents plopped on the dirty floor speckled with pools of transmission fluid the color of old blood, spare parts sitting in motor oil to flake off the rust.

"I don't need the stuff you don't want," Cassie said. "The stuff you were going to throw out." Her eyes flashed. "I'm not a charity case."

But Silas was already pouncing on a shirt. It was a soft cotton, useless in the mountains.

Cassie looked at Silas, already buttoning up the shirt. Her face softened. "Cotton kills, you know," she said. "Get it wet in the mountains and you die." She scooped up the pile of clothes and set it carefully on a lawn chair. "If you really can't wear these, we might as well do you a favor and take them."

The shirt was too big for Silas, but he refused to take it off. He rolled up the sleeves, the hem falling almost to his knees.

"We're clean," Cassie said. She stuck out her chin. "Or we jump in the river. That's better anyway. And then in the winter we sneak in the RV park shower if someone's propped open the door."

"The laundromat has a shower too, but you have to pay in quarters, and the water doesn't last more than a minute per quarter," Silas said. "That's only for emergencies."

"Don't you dare feel sorry for us," Cassie said. "We won't stand for it."

"I don't," Lina said quickly. But she had seen how Cassie's eyes glittered when the light hit them. There was more to Cassie than she had ever imagined, just like there was with Silas, layers and layers of her. Lina wondered how long it would take to get down to her core. And then she wondered why she wanted to get there. She just knew that she did.

"Take a tool," Cassie said, indicating a pile of rusty implements in the corner.

Cassie picked up a long whip-like saw and an iron bar. Silas grabbed a combination axe and hoe. Lina took the only recognizable tool, a shovel.

They left right from the shop, stepping from the sunlit road to the gloom of the forest. Cassie looked over her shoulder. "You have to be careful," she said. "I've never seen anyone up here, but sometimes I feel like somebody is watching. Always look before you go in."

Lina looked back too, but there was only what there always was, tin-roofed buildings simmering in the sun, nobody in sight. Immediately they started to climb, pushing through clumps of waist-high scratchy bushes. She hurried to follow the others, slipping in her Chukka boots, still the only walking shoes that she had.

The trees struggled to survive up here, locked in a battle with each other. The forest had not burned in a hundred years, and the loggers hadn't been allowed in since it had been declared a wilderness back in the sixties. The difference between this place and the Chalks was pronounced. The Chalks roller-coasted gently over glacial moraines, the trails dipping in and out of clustered white fir thickets and onto spacious ridges. In the Chalks, you could see the sky.

Here in the Isolations, all she could see was darkness. Even though it was afternoon, the trees battled for sunlight, blocking it from reaching the ground. Decades of pine needles lay in deep piles under her feet. Nothing could grow in the gloom of the forest floor. The slope they climbed tilted steeply above her head. Large rocks, the kind her father called glacial erratics, tilted dangerously, and she imagined them tumbling down toward her, pancaking her flat. The whole impression was that the dark forest didn't want any of them in there. That they didn't belong and never would.

She almost turned around. She watched Cassie and Silas scramble like monkeys up an incline while she clawed her way after them. They never looked back, and Lina wasn't sure that she could find her way down if she didn't keep up. The thought of being out there alone, the whole forest uniform in its sameness, kept her going. The only choice was to keep up.

After what could have been an hour or ten minutes, Cassie stopped to wait for her.

"Here is where we go," she said. "Dodge around this blowdown. But don't all of you go the same route, ever. We can't leave a path."

They divided up as they headed around a head-high stack of blown-down trees, their tops still green, Silas and Lina on one side, Cassie on the other, and then, suddenly, they were standing on a trail. But this was no tourist trail, worn down to bedrock from passing feet. When Lina had walked those trails, dust rose in huge clouds. The bones of trees lay exposed as the trails expanded from people trying to avoid mud or water or wanted to walk side by side. Those trails seemed to spear through the woods, breaking the forest in two.

In contrast this trail looked meant for elves, a thin brown line snaking into the forest. The canopy stretched overhead, and branches reached out across the trail, forming a tunnel. The forest hugged the trail rather than the trail bullying its way through. Lina was instantly enchanted.

"What is this?" she asked. "How did it get here?"

"This is what we call a ghost trail," Cassie explained. "This is how we keep them. Just wide enough for us to get through."

Walking down the trail, she realized, the three of them were like the deer, flowing through the easy points and going around the hard ones, working with the land instead of against it.

"See why we do it?" Silas asked. "We have a bunch of others just like this one."

"Aren't you worried someone will find them?"

"Nah. People don't take the hard way. They won't go into the Isolations. They believe all the stories. Sometimes I watch tourists as they go into the Chalks. They march up the trail without even noticing what's beside them. I've sat on a cliff right up above them and nobody even noticed I was there."

"How do you build them? The trails?"

"This is the main trail we use," Cassie said. "We have others that branch off this one. If you really want to know how to build trails, we'll teach you. Come on, we stop about a mile up ahead. We'll start there."

They arrived at a place where the noticeable trail faded into a wall of brush.

"This needs a lot of work," Cassie said. "Brushing. Cutting. Water bars."

Lina leaned on her shovel, watching Silas begin to dig in the hard soil.

"How did you learn how to do this?"

"We did it wrong a lot. I got a book from the library that told us how to do it. But mostly we make it up as we go. The trail tells us what it needs."

"How does it do that?"

"It's easy, once you know what the trail is trying to tell you," Cassie said. "See here? This is what the book calls the fall line. It's the shortest way down the mountain. So, you build the trail here, right?"

Lina nodded. "Right."

"Wrong! That's the lazy way. See how the water has run down the mountain the same way as the fall line? Water takes the easiest route, just like people. If the water runs down your trail, it eats away at it. Pretty soon your trail is gone." Instead, Cassie said, you built switchbacks, or climbing turns, whichever the land would allow. You let the water do what it wanted by putting in water bars, rock or wood structures placed deep in the tread to divert any flow off the trail.

"A lot of the time, the miners or the cowboys just blazed up the hills the easiest way. They just wanted to get to the top. That's where we take the ghost trails and make them better. They'll last this way. We add on a switchback, or build a dip, or move it altogether. But we try to keep the bones of the trail the way it was. We try to meet up with it again as soon as we can."

Most trees that fell across the trail, they left if they could step over them. But occasionally there were behemoths, three or four feet around, brought down by rot or snow or wind. Those, Cassie said, they should cut.

From somewhere, Cassie had procured an ancient crosscut saw. Lina knew enough not to ask where.

"They don't make them like this anymore," Cassie said,

running her fingers gingerly over the teeth. "The loggers used to use these before chainsaws came along. They called them misery whips, for reasons you can guess. But isn't it glorious?"

The saw was as tall as Silas, and had two wooden handles, one at each end. Lina knelt on one side of an enormous fallen tree, Silas on the other.

"Don't pull it so hard," Silas ordered. "The saw doesn't care if you're strong. You push it toward me, but gently, and I take it and push it back. You don't force it. When you do it right, you can hear the saw sing."

Chunks of yellow flesh dropped from the cut and deep shudders ran through the log as it cracked far in its heart. Silas stopped and pounded a plastic wedge in the open mouth they had made. "Stops the bind," he said. "The tree could close right up on the saw, and we'd never be able to get it out. The wedge keeps it open, see?"

They sawed for a while, shavings falling from the tree and coating her skin.

"Listen," Silas said. "Hear that? That's the saw singing." Lina listened and he was right; as one of them pulled the saw back and the other reached for it, the saw hummed.

❖ ❖ ❖

"Do you really like doing this?" Lina whispered to Silas as Cassie went off to scout for the remnants of the old trail.

He shrugged. "I like working on cars better, but before we started doing this, Cassie wasn't the way she is now. This makes her happy. I was scared before, the way she was. She was always boiling. You know, like a pot of water on a stove ... you never knew when she was going to boil over ...

and you sure didn't want to be anywhere near when she did. She's better now that she is out here."

Winter was impossible, he said. Cassie hated it, cooped up inside, the trails drifted over with snow. That was when she went a little crazy. He liked escaping to the relative safety of school.

"I sit by the smoker's gate and all those guys are just listening to their radios and bumming cigarettes and it's peaceful up there. Don't get me wrong, Cassie wouldn't hurt anyone except herself."

Lina glanced up the trail, but Cassie was still too far ahead to hear. "What does that mean?"

"I probably shouldn't say," Silas answered with a guilty look on his face. "I mean, that's private. But she's either bouncing off the walls with projects, like, let's make some shelves, get out the welding torch and make something over here, she never stops. It makes me dizzy sometimes. And then other times, she won't move ... tells me the air weighs too much. So, I'm always glad when we can get out on the trails again."

Trail work was the hardest thing that Lina had ever done, particularly building water bars. They used what was available. Rocks or stout pieces of wood, or sometimes they would just dig a trench, though that wasn't as good, because those filled in fast with debris, or clogged up, pooling the water in one place.

Sweat running like a river down her face, Lina swung half-heartedly at the implacable ground. It was stubborn, resisting her efforts. Ghost trails? Why was she even doing this? She could be anywhere else. Somewhere in town, Molly and the rest of the girls were wearing sundresses, the coolness of popsicles lingering on their tongues. They would be wearing makeup to cover their real faces: pale beige Cover Girl foundation spackled on heavy; bright blue eyeshadow, a touch of powder blush, toenails burnished to a pink sheen. But she hated that even more. Lina stabbed the shovel into the dirt.

"If you can't do it right, don't bother," Cassie snapped. "Go on home where you belong." She tossed her mass of hair over her shoulder. "You aren't tough enough to do this."

Her words stung. Again, Lina thought of the girls down below.

"I don't belong down there," Lina countered.

"Yes, you do," Cassie said. She planted her feet on the trail and stared Lina down. "You have a mother, right? You have food in the fridge and a bed to sleep in. I bet you even have a dishwasher. Maybe a microwave. Nobody hurts you there. Nobody comes in your room when you don't want them to. See what I'm saying? Maybe that's where you should be instead of out here with us."

"I want to be here," Lina blurted out. She was struck by how easy it was here, compared to down below. Here were Cassie and Silas, who plopped into the dirt, belched unapologetically, and shoveled sandwiches into their mouths with filthy fingers. Wasn't that better, just to be who you were? She wiped her nose on her sleeve. "I'll do it right."

Cassie sighed. "I don't get it, Tag. If I had what you had ..." Her voice trailed off. "Okay. Maybe take a break from the water bars and work on clearing the brush. But use those loppers like you mean it. Brush is the beginning of the end. Once this bristly stuff, see it? Once it takes over the trail, it's pretty much gone forever. We have to cut it back, not way back, but back enough so we can get through. We have to be relentless. Got it?"

Lina nodded. Silas crabbed back to where she stood.

"Don't take it personal," he whispered under the sound of his loppers. He threw a leafy branch off the trail. "It's only because she cares so much about these trails."

"Why?" Lina glanced up at Cassie's retreating back, swinging the rock bar with determination as she climbed. "Why does she care so much? It's just a trail. Nobody's going to hike it but us."

"Beats me," he said, closing the mouth of the loppers around a stout limb. "Maybe she thinks that it's one thing that belongs to her."

"Nobody owns a trail."

"Not true," Silas said, moving away from her. "We own these. They're ours."

Lina studied the intent on his face as he chose which plants lived or died.

❖ ❖ ❖

Though each day Lina told herself she wouldn't go back to the shop, that this was the day that she would find Molly and the other girls, each morning she found herself retracing her steps back up Nip and Tuck. Though she couldn't put it into words, she was drawn back there, almost as if a magnet was pulling her. Maybe it was crawling with Silas under a car, the thrill that shot through her when they tucked the last part into the gaping mouth of the engine, even though the truck still wouldn't run, and Lina was suspecting it never would. Maybe it was the trails after all, when she turned and looked back at a smooth stretch of tread that they had spent all day digging and clearing, dipping away into the forest. Maybe it was Cassie and Silas themselves.

"Will you cut my hair?" Silas asked.

"I like your hair long," Cassie interrupted. She crossed her arms and swung her foot. "Anyways, I'll cut it if you want. Why are you having her do it?"

Silas shrugged. "Maybe she won't cut my ears like you always do."

"Wimp." Cassie grinned. "As if I want to touch your nasty hair anyway. Have at it, Tag. I'm off to get some wood for us to burn when it gets cold."

Lina stood behind Silas, brushing his hair flat. His hair was so fine that it slid through her fingers. It was an entirely different texture than his sister's. Cassie's looked like she could never force a comb through her curls.

"Why don't you tell Cassie about how the kids treat you at school?"

Silas shrugged. "I don't need looking after. The last thing I want is her to come in there and try to kick some ass. Like I'm a baby and can't stand up for myself. You've noticed, right? Cass is kind of like an avalanche. She takes out everything in her path. Sometimes that can be good, but sometimes it can be not what you want."

He was right. Lina wouldn't have told her either. She moved slowly around the chair, snipping uneven pieces of blond hair, thinking about avalanches. Sometimes she could see slides from town, the snow gathering itself up in one place and then thundering down a chute in an explosion of white, almost like a wave breaking on land. There were supposed to be ways that you could watch out for avalanches, her father had told her. Days when feet of snow had fallen all at once, when strong winds raked the cornices up high, but mostly you had to know what lay beneath each layer. There was sometimes a weaker tier buried under the new ones, he had said, and the only way to know was to dig deep to find it. It all sounded mysterious to Lina. Basically, it seemed that you just held your breath, crossed your fingers, and hoped for the best.

Silas looked like a different boy when she was done, a fringe of hair across his forehead, the rest falling just above his shoulders. She could see his eyes, and the color made her stop and stare. She had never seen that shade of blue in anyone's face except for Cassie's. It was light, almost translucent, like aquamarine.

"There," she said. "What do you think?" Too late, she noticed there was no mirror, but Silas just ran his hands through his shorter hair and seemed satisfied.

"My mother used to cut my hair," he said. "But she wasn't very good at it. She would cut one side too short and so she had to keep cutting to make it look even. Usually, I ended up with a buzz cut. I'm not sure why she couldn't cut straight. It's not that hard."

"Drunk," Cassie said. She had come in and dropped some split wood on the floor. "Courtesy of the Berghdals," she said. "Nice dry fir."

"Where is she now? Your mom?"

Silas shrugged. "Don't know."

"Don't care," Cassie added.

Lina swept up a pile of gold hair. "Where did she go?"

"Beats me," Silas said. "She was just there one day and when we got home from school, she wasn't. I kept thinking she was going to come back. She never even said anything, not a single word."

Cassie crouched on her heels, stacking wood. "That's not what happened, Silas. She didn't want to be a mom anymore.

Said she was only forty and was wasting her pretty years in this valley. Said that it wasn't personal, but that she had to go and find herself. I guess she must have been really lost because she never has come back."

"My dad left this spring," Lina said. "Looking for a treasure. It's stupid. It always feels like he chose the treasure over us."

"Hunter Malone," Cassie said. "I heard that wasn't real. That the guy did it to see how many people fall for it. Nobody around here believes it's true."

Cassie rooted around in a milk crate. "You can't keep wearing those boots. You're falling all the time. Try these. They belonged to our mother, but I think they'll fit."

Lina slid on the old boots, molded to another woman's foot. She watched Cassie carefully refold a sheet back in the tote. She caught her breath. It had been obvious all along, but she hadn't wanted to see it. She had somehow thought they just hung out here for the day and went back to a real house, even though there had been plenty of clues to prove otherwise. The bedrolls in the corner, a camp stove on one bench, the way Silas and Cassie always seemed to be in the building, never at any other home.

"Wait, you're living here?" Lina asked.

"Just because we want to," Cassie said. Her eyes dared Lina to contradict her. "We could live a lot of different places if we wanted to. We like it here. Nobody bothers us."

"It belongs to our dad free and clear," Silas piped up. "Nobody's going to take it away from us. Unless you tell."

"I won't tell. Why would I tell?"

"Everybody tells," Silas said. "That's why I don't really talk in school. You can't trust anybody. It's not normal to live in a shop. If they found out, they'd move us out of the valley …

separate us. So, zip it at school."

"Are we done talking about this?" Cassie asked. She grabbed her backpack. "Let's go. We have a lot of ground to cover."

As they hiked up the ghost trail, Silas fell back to walk just behind Lina. Usually he was out in front, maintaining a big gap between them. "That's not really true, what she said," he confided. "We used to live in a house, but we lost it."

How could you lose a house? Lina imagined a building lifted by winds, tossed into the river.

"When my dad left, there wasn't anybody to pay for it," Silas explained. "So, we lost it. Some other family is living there now."

Their father left them money sometimes, Silas said. That was how they bought food. And wood was mostly free. That is, the way Cassie went about it. She would whistle herself past someone's wood stack, checking to see if anyone was home, and take one or two pieces. And, according to Silas, she never took from the same place more than once a week.

Lina stopped in the middle of the trail. "That's stealing!"

"Shh, she'll hear you. And it's not really stealing. Cassie says it's more like extended borrowing. Anyway, she said she has her eye on a chainsaw that nobody's using. Once we have that, we can come up here and cut our own wood. Don't get your panties in a twist." He hoisted his shovel over his shoulder and increased the pace. "Why are you such a slowpoke? Come on."

Lina followed him, her thoughts jumbled. She thought of her house, with rows of canned food lined up in the pantry, the wood pile out back covered with a blue tarp. The loft she and her sister slept in, books on shelves, more clothes in their closets than she could possibly wear. Those satin jackets, that had cost a month's allowance. Though her parents had spent all the money they had on their house on the hill, they were rich compared to Silas and Cassie, who slept on a concrete floor and had to choose between warmth and trouble. It felt uneasy, considering the gap between them and her family.

Lina knew she could bring them old clothes and cut Silas' hair, but deep down that wouldn't change who they were and what the future held for them. It was expected that Lina would go to college, because her parents had, and because that was what you did in a family like hers. What did that leave for kids like Silas and Cassie? It seemed that they got what was left when everyone else was done.

❖ ❖ ❖

On the third day they built rock walls. Most people wouldn't even bother, Cassie said, not for these kinds of trails. "But look here." She pointed at the upward side. "See here? See how undercut this is getting? If we don't do anything here, the trail gets narrower and narrower, all this dirt pouring down the mountain when it rains. It needs a barrier. So, we build a wall."

A rock wall sounded hard to Lina. "Can't we just dig farther back into the hillside?"

"In some places you can." She grabbed a handful of dirt in her palm. "Look at this, though. See how it crumbles when I make a fist? It'll just keep crumbling no matter how far we dig. A wall is the only solution."

Cassie noted Lina's blank expression.

"Listen up, Lina. We need to make sure we pay attention to the heart of the wall. Hearting means the small stones that fill in the gaps the big stones leave. It's the most important part of the entire wall. If you don't pay attention to it, the whole wall will be weak. The heart is everything."

Lina picked up a rock and studied it. "It's really called hearting?"

"Some people call it backfill, but I like hearting instead. Because the big rocks, the outer ones, are what forms the wall, like your feet and your head and your brain. But the little ones are what matter the most. Like your heart."

She stumbled under the weight of the largest rocks, the ones Cassie said were called keystones ... the foundation. They dug with stolen tools into the slope, creating a space for the keystones.

"Then you make tiers, like layers in a cake," Cassie said. "Don't just pile the next layer on top of the other. They have to be overlapping. That makes them stronger."

The final layer, Cassie said, was often called the capstone. Those rocks had to be perfect because the top layer had to be completely stable. She judged every rock that Silas and Lina staggered up with. "Not flat enough," she would say, shaking her head. "Not big enough. Try again."

It took them another three days to build one retaining wall. When they were done, it wasn't big, ten feet wide, and only up to Lina's waist, but it was strong and sturdy. "This wall is going to last forever," Cassie said. "A hundred years from now, it's going to still be here."

Lina glanced back at the wall she had helped build as they gathered their tools and headed down the mountain. There was something that felt permanent about what she had done, leaving her mark in the wilderness. She knew that what Cassie had said was only partially true, because she had seen the remnants of other walls, built by other people, on the tourist trails in the Chalks. Rain, wind and snow worked together to create cracks in the heart of those walls, sending supporting rocks tumbling down, compromising their integrity. Still, the outlines remained, even when the heart was gone. Anyone walking by their new wall could see what was left. They would know that someone had meant business.

❖ ❖ ❖

"I got a chainsaw," Cassie said one day. Leroy down at the gas station let me have some oil and gas for it too." She flourished a red container.

"Where did you get the saw?"

"Better you don't know."

"You stole it," Lina said. "Cassie, someone's going to be after you for this one."

"It's just borrowing, Tag," she said. "We'll put it back when we're done with it."

"Won't people hear it and wonder what we're doing?"

"Not if we're careful. We only run it high on the mountain, and we only do it during the day, when there's enough noise down in town to muffle it. Anyway, you know what the Isolations are like. You could stand fifteen feet away in some places and holler at the top of your lungs and nobody would hear you. How do you think the wolves have survived this long?"

Lina still hadn't heard the wolves, but with Cassie and Silas, she had found secrets in the Isolations, secrets she was sure nobody else had ever discovered.

❖ ❖ ❖

The secret—what nobody else knew—was beyond the melancholy morainal hills, deep into the dark sun-starved forest, where Cassie, Silas, and Lina could climb into the heart of the place, where the mountain range opened.

It was an amazing sight, with little pocket lakes nestled in rings of limestone, pure white rock and sky-colored water. Long, sweet ridge walks, lined with showy big-petaled flowers that were the same color as the sun, where they would often be walking above the clouds, the valley below shrouded in a white blanket. In other places, basalt cliffs stretched unbroken from earth to clouds. Raptors with red wings that she could hear in the silence as they flapped from one outcrop to another. Elk, grazing in the pocket meadows. Once, a cinnamon-colored bear, standing two-legged to watch for danger as they passed by.

Basalt, granite, and limestone weren't supposed to be in one mountain range; she knew that from school, but the Isolations were like that, a contradiction. There weren't supposed to be the things they found there, mixed up rocks that belonged elsewhere, moose and deer and elk all in one valley. There were plants here, Silas said, that he was pretty sure didn't exist anywhere else on earth. At least, he said, he had never seen any in the plant books in the library, or in the Chalks.

One day they discovered a river. Lina had been hearing it for hours as they worked toward it, a steady grumble in the distance. Even Silas and Cassie had never been this far out on the spur trail they were creating. The trail seemed to lead to the river, and Cassie said it probably did, since water was the lifeblood that everyone and everything needed. Finally, they broke out through head-high willow onto the sloping banks of the river. As wide across as Lina was tall, the river flowed lazily through a bed of egg-shaped rocks that were the same color as the sun. It was not a coincidence, Lina thought, that so many things that lived in the earth copied the sun. Like water, the sun was the other thing that everyone needed.

"What is this river?" she asked. She knelt to dip a hand, which instantly went numb. "Where does it go?"

"It's ours," Silas said. "You can name it if you want." They had named a lot of things in the Isolations—flowers, peaks, lakes.

"Really? I can name it?" Lina noticed how the river leapt as it hit rocks mid-stream. Some of the rocks were carried along with the water, tumbling like thunder as they went.

"Dancing River," she said.

Silas rolled his eyes. "Oh, brother, last time we let you name anything." He grinned. "Dancing River it is."

They had reached the end of the trail and there was nowhere else to go but across. Cassie pointed to the other side, where the trees were thinned slightly, an opening that might be where the trail picked up again.

"Here's how you cross a river," Cassie said. "Watch and learn." Lina copied her, how she shuffled her feet along the bottom, through the slippery stones. You started upstream of where you wanted to go, Cassie said, and aimed higher up than you meant to land. "Whatever you do," she said, "don't freeze in the middle of the river. Go back or keep going forward, but not making a decision could kill you."

Once they were across the river, Cassie offered more advice. "If you can, you always want to cross on logs to avoid clammy feet sloshing around in boots."

Scouting up and down the riverbank, Cassie spotted a tree that had fallen across the river at helpful angles.

"It's easy, you chicken," she said. "Put your feet at an angle. Not straight like that. Put them out. Then you just walk. Don't look down at the water. Don't ever look down."

"But we're on the other side," Lina said, her feet tingling in her boots, just beginning to wake up. "We don't need to cross back yet."

"Practice," Cassie said. "What would you do if I weren't here? I won't always be around, you know. Try crossing it once. See how you do. And then we'll come back."

Silas scampered across easily at a dead run, making a joke of it, windmilling his arms and yelling as if he were about to fall. Lina placed a trembling leg on the log and held out her arms at a stiff angle, certain that every step would be her last. She glanced down at the river below her. Crossing on foot, the river had seemed benign, just shin height. Now, above it on a five-inch platform, she noticed the sharpness of the rocks below and imagined herself cartwheeling from the log, landing headfirst in the water.

"Don't look down," Cassie called. "Don't look at the water. That will make you fall for sure."

Lina forced her gaze back upward. Sliding each foot tentatively forward, she lurched to the other side where Cassie was waiting. "Unbuckle your backpack, you goof," she said. "If you fall in the river, its weight will hold you down. You'll drown. Don't you know anything?"

"Why can't we just build a bridge?" Lina asked. She wondered how she would ever get back to the other side. She resolved to wade. Logs were too uncertain.

"You don't want to make it easy," Silas said. "Then it would be just like the Chalks."

Lina learned from Cassie that a trail was like a river.

"You size up the landscape," she said. "You look for how water flows across it, how the rivers drain to the valley and where the rain goes when it falls. You grab a handful of soil and crumble it in your fingers, seeing what kind it is ... clay, will that hold a trail? If the dirt doesn't stick together, it would be better to go higher, or lower. Mid-slope was often better than down in the lowlands. You have to work with the land, Lina."

Of course, Cassie always had more.

"You never go through the meadows if you can help it: trails there can turn into impassible bogs. You want most often to stick to the treed slopes, circling the mountain to get higher or lower. And you can't just charge up the mountain in a hurry. You must be patient, work your way up. Listen, Lina, steep grades aren't good, because they will erode, turning your tread into slick ball-bearings under your feet."

Lina always had the feeling she should be taking notes.

"The land tells you where to build a trail," Cassie continued. "It isn't always the easiest way or forcing your way through. That's the problem with most people. They try to bully it into submission. It might work for a while, but the land always fights back. If you go on some of the hiking trails, the ones the tourists walk, you'll see big ruts carved out in the meadows, higher than your waist sometimes. Trails taken out by avalanches because someone took the easy way when they built them. Trails sliding off the mountain because they went too high on the shoulder, or in the wrong kind of soil. Or water has found its way onto the trail, because if it can, it always will."

Wrestling a timber into a shallow grave to make a water bar, Lina looked ahead to where Cassie and Silas were doing the same thing. The sight of them all in a line made her throat hurt just a little, enough to make her swallow hard. That summer they had become her family, closer to her than her own ever was. She didn't want to give them up, not ever.

Cassie talked about the trails as if they were people she

loved. She had names for all of them, names that described their attributes. There was the Belt, a trail that wound around the waist of a nameless, tree-shrouded mountain as if it were cinching up the peak's trousers. The Bighorn Basin Trail led to a rock-rimmed saucer of permanent snow where she and Silas had once watched dun-colored animals pour off the cliffs. Frosty Meadow dead-ended in a high cirque that was never, ever warm.

Silas had even drawn a map of the trails they had been on, including trails he was sure they were yet to find.

"Yep, there's others out there," Cassie agreed. "Other trails to be found and restored. Someday, it will be the way it used to be."

You didn't argue with Cassie, but Lina knew that everything would change. Her father had shown her the places on their land where old fires had gone through, decades before. You could tell by the catfaces in the trees, he said, pointing out the scars deep in the bark, old wounds nearly healed over. Wilderness was made to change, he said, meadows becoming forests, rivers changing course. What chance did a trail, just a two-foot-wide piece of cleared ground, stand against that? But Cassie believed, and Lina wanted to believe in something, so she went along with it.

They hoisted stolen tools from unguarded sheds, and hiked up into the mountains. They slung piles of brush artfully across the trail openings so nobody would see where their work began. They had to do this, Cassie said, because the rangers would shut them down if they knew what they were up to. Why didn't they just go to them and ask permission, Lina wanted to know. Surely, the forest service would welcome the help. The seasonal trail crew stuck to the Chalks, strictly cut and run, not able to keep up with anything other than fallen trees.

"We're what they call trail vigilantes," Cassie laughed. "They don't want us up here. They want the old trails to be forgotten."

On the trails, Lina realized that she had learned to love the wilderness. It wasn't like anywhere else, the strangeness of school, the dark confines of her house, three women all wanting something different and unnamed. Back there, and in the real world, it seemed that the role of women was to want and wait. They couldn't seize life into their own hands and stride with it.

Out here, it didn't matter how she looked, or what she wore. She had grown strong enough to take an axe and chop out the heart of a tree until it broke apart in two halves, and then she could put her back into it and roll it off the trail, watching it tumble down through the trees below. She was free in a way she had never felt before. This freedom always lasted until they came out to the road. Cassie and Silas darted back into the shop, making sure nobody was watching, and she faced the long walk home, where nothing was ever different.

"Hey," Silas said. "Look. I think this is a wolf track."

Lina came over to where he stood. A footprint, larger than a dog's, pressed into the fresh dirt of a water bar they had dug the day before. She met his eyes and a spark leapt between them.

"The wolves were here?"

"We've heard them, I told you. Plenty of times."

Lina thought she could feel the breath of wolves, inches from where she stood.

"Do you think they're watching us now?"

"Maybe. They only come out when they want to. Maybe we'll see one once we go to the Floor. That's the only place we've ever heard them."

"It's glorious to sit up there and hear them," Cassie added. "We've never seen them, but I always think we will one day."

Cassie and Silas had been talking about the Floor for weeks. They would go there, they said, once they got a certain number of miles done. What Lina knew and what they didn't say was that she had to pass a test, though what that test was, they had never said. The Floor was special. They had never taken anyone there before. She had to earn it.

"Let's go today," Cassie said. "We're already halfway there anyway."

Because Cassie could change her mind in an instant, Lina threw her loppers in a patch of low brush and followed. She couldn't hide her grin. She was finally going to see the place they had talked about, the place they said was the most special. She wasn't sure what it was, but she knew from the way Silas and Cassie talked about it that it was the last, big secret. Knowing about the Floor meant she belonged.

They walked the remains of an old trail, one that they hadn't cleared yet. They had been saving this one, Silas told her, because it was the most important. They had to practice on the others, to see what worked and what didn't. They didn't want to screw this one up, he said. Once you did, it was hard to go back.

The old trail had sunk back into the forest, only a faint depression showing where it had been. As they walked, Cassie pointed out the signs. Old cut logs, their butt ends extending into the trail, the bark weathered silver. Blazes nearly healed over at head height. Places where switchbacks had been carved out of the flesh of the mountain. It was easy if you knew what to look for, she said. It was like putting a puzzle together. Someday, she said, they would have a real trail up here. "Maybe this summer, if it lasts long enough."

Cassie stopped to take a long drink from the water bottle she had filled from the river. "Almost here," she said. "It's a mean climb, but it's worth it. You'll see."

Lina was starting to think they would never get there, following behind Cassie in her old black skirt and Silas in his torn jeans, when they crested a ridge, just another in a long series of pine-clad ridges, and Cassie stopped short. They had come to a clearing entirely circled by trees, a small pocket of grass that was able to make a stand because sometime, years ago, somebody had cleared the woods here. In the middle of the clearing, was a flat slab made of rough-cut wood, supported by cinder blocks.

"What is this place?" Lina breathed, turning in a circle. It seemed magical, as if it had grown here all on its own.

"We don't know. We just call it the Floor. Found it by accident, found pieces of this old trail and followed it up here. Sometime, years ago, who knows how long, maybe twenty years ago, somebody built that trail. They started to build a cabin here. This is as far as they got."

Lina imagined someone climbing the mountain, stepping over downed logs and pushing through brush to find this one perfect spot. From here, once someone had been able to see the whole world, their backs against the sheltering forest. Someone had cut down some of the ancient trees by hand and built a rough floor. They had certainly intended to return, Lina thought, but something had happened. Over time, small trees had grown tall, the clearing beginning to fill in. Whose place this had been was unknown, Silas said. Maybe the Forest Service had known at one time, but the old records had been long lost. It had been absorbed into the wilderness. It was likely, Silas said, that nobody knew about this place but them.

"I knew you would love it," Cassie said. She stood in the middle of the clearing, the only place the sun stayed. It fell in a thick column and covered her face, turning her hair into a mass of gold. The rest of the clearing only got a passing glance of light, the trees thick enough to block most direct sunlight. Why someone would climb so high and so far from where others lived was a mystery.

"I come up here a lot," Cassie said. "I sleep up here sometimes."

"Aren't you afraid to sleep up here alone?"

"Afraid? No way. Up here, it's the safest I've ever felt. Silas and I make up stories about this place. Someone wanted this place bad, wanted it enough to haul the lumber up here. If you look, you can see where they cut trees to make space. But you can tell they thought about each tree, and they didn't take all the ones they could have taken."

"I think maybe it was two people," Silas said. "A man and woman, who hiked up here one day and decided this would be the perfect place. They would stay up here forever and nobody in town would ever know what happened to them."

"Then what happened?"

He shrugged. "Don't know. Maybe one of them changed their mind. Said the snow was too deep. Said it was too far of a walk. That they would starve up here, or the wolves would eat them."

"That's dumb," Cassie said. "I wouldn't let anyone keep me from living up here. I think it was a woman who wanted to get away from everyone else. She came up here all alone and sat right here where I'm sitting, and it was the first time she could really breathe."

"Why didn't she come back to finish the cabin, then?"

"She died before she could make it back," Cassie said. "Or something like that."

They sat on the platform, drinking from their water bottles. Up here, the wind was softer, broken by the trees. The snow would pile up here, Lina thought. It would drift as high as the roof of a cabin. It would be peaceful, buried deep in snow.

"I can hear her talking sometimes," Cassie said. "The woman who built this. I know it was a woman."

"What does she say?"

"I can't just tell you," Cassie said. "That's too easy. You have to try to listen for yourself."

Lina listened as hard as she could, but all she could make out was the gentle buzz of insects as they flew through the pine-scented air. A white-tipped butterfly bumbled past and landed briefly on the rough wood next to her. When she moved, it flew away.

Silas went off to check a spring he said he knew about, taking their empty water bottles with him. Lina sat next to Cassie on the slab, their bare feet dangling off the edge, boots discarded below. A storm was coming; Lina could hear the distant rumble of thunder in the distance. With the passing of the calendar into August, the threat of thunderstorms had increased. Nearly every day the clouds stacked high into the sky. So far it had just been build-up, no relief from the sticky air.

"We'd better go down," Lina said.

Cassie didn't seem concerned. "I was struck by lightning once. Haven't you heard the saying? Lightning doesn't strike in the same place twice. We're good here."

Lina stared at her. "What? You were struck by lightning? How?"

"Oh, it's not that interesting," she said. "Just another lightning story. A lot of people have them."

"Tell me."

"Oh, all right," she said. "If you really want to know. It was on the Devil's Staircase. You know how you can't see the storms from the west until they're on top of you? The mountains block them. That's where it happened."

The sky had gotten darker than a new bruise, and the woods had grown still, that kind of hush Lina sensed happened right before a storm hit. It also seemed to her that if she sat very still and didn't speak, she would learn something important.

Cassie leaned back, closing her eyes. Her voice was slow, the words sliding out one at a time. "Silas and me, we were climbing up. It was the first time we had been up there. We were going pretty slow, because we didn't really know the way. Kept getting cliffed out. Silas, he would follow me anywhere, so he wouldn't quit. I knew if I called it, he would turn around. He didn't care. If you haven't noticed, Silas likes to go with the flow. It wouldn't bother him, make the top or not, all the same. But I cared. I wanted to make it to the top. And we did. But when we got up there, the storm was already there."

"What did you do then?"

"You know something, Tag? The doctors said that when you've been struck by lightning, everything about you changes. The person you become, they said, was not the person you had been. I literally became someone different."

"Cassie, what happened? Tell me what happened."

"A lightning bolt warms the nearby air nearly five times hotter than the surface of the sun. Just think about it, Tag, that heat ripping through your skin, your bones. It's as if the sun comes and swallows you up and spits you out. Of course, it has to change you. Your brain can actually boil inside its skull!"

There were so few who made it, Cassie said, as if she were a member of a special lightning survivor's club.

"Your straight hair can spring up curly or turn white overnight," she explained. "You can be swept by sudden rage when you were once calm or become swamped by eternal tears when before you were made of stone. Your body can betray you in a lot of ways. You can develop a permanent twitch or lose your sight. Lightning can also stop your heart forever. I'm just lucky."

Cassie laughed. "Silas saved me," she continued. "He was only ten then, but he saved me. He ran for help. I stopped breathing. I actually died, Tag, I died. But I decided to come back."

Lina let out her own breath. "Really?"

"It's like I'm daring it to come back, sometimes. I mean, how often do you get so close to dying? How often do you get to make the choice to come back?"

She rolled up her sleeve. "This what the lightning left behind. The doctors said it would fade, but it hasn't."

An intricate design spiraled across her arm as if someone had taken a dark pen and drawn long, sweeping strokes, one main trunk with branches feathering from it. It was what the lightning had left, showing its path through her body.

Another rumble of thunder cascaded across the sky. Not so close. Not yet.

"The fancy name for them is Lichtenberg figures," Cassie said. "It comes from the blood vessels bursting under my skin from the electricity. Sometimes people call them lightning flowers. I like that name better, don't you?"

"It looks like a tree," Lina said. "Not a flower."

Flowers were much too delicate for whatever this was. This was strong, undeniable.

"Do you want to touch it?" Cassie asked.

Lina hesitated. Girls weren't supposed to touch other girls, not the way she did when she was little. When she was six, she had wound her arm around the waists of other girls. They had held hands as they skipped down the street. But at some point, that became unacceptable.

"It doesn't mean you love me," Cassie said impatiently. "Just touch it. Tell me if you feel anything."

Lina had thought that the flowers would feel painted on her skin, but instead her fingers felt raised bumps. She traced the outline of the lightning mark as long as she dared. She was reading Cassie like a map, Lina thought, learning who she was.

"Can you feel it?" Cassie asked. "The lightning? It's still in there. Trapped. Looking for a way out."

Lina thought if she tried hard enough, she could feel it, a faint sizzle under her fingers, as though Cassie still burned somewhere deep inside.

She could hear Silas whistling through the trees as he approached them. He always whistled the same tune, something that sounded familiar but that she could not place. Once he showed up, they would head back down the trail. Cassie would roll down her sleeve and never speak of it again. "Don't mention this to Silas," she said. "He doesn't like to remember it. He's thirteen, but he's really just a kid. I want him to stay that way as long as he can."

"At school," Lina began, but then she stopped herself. She had promised Silas she wouldn't say anything. Instead, she said, "He saved your life."

"Of course," Cassie said. "He's saved my life a bunch of times, and I've saved his. That's what we do for each other. We're all each other has."

Lina tried to imagine Rainy saving her life. She still would, wouldn't she? Rainy spent most of her time at Danny's now, only coming home at night, well after dinner. Lina would fix herself a plate and go up to her room, waiting until morning when she could see Cassie and Silas again.

"I'd do it for you, Tag," Cassie said. "Save your life, I mean. I would. If I were dying, if I needed you, would you save mine?" Lina hugged her knees. The first drops of rain filtered down through the trees, burrowing into her skin like small needles, but Cassie didn't seem to notice.

"Of course, I would," Lina said, although what Cassie was asking was too far off and strange to understand. There would never be an occasion where this was needed. They were young, their muscles hardened from the trails. It would be years before they would have to think about saving the other's life.

"You better," Cassie said. "Because when I show people this place, and my arm, they become my family. That means something. Not the messed-up family I was born into, but the family I choose."

Silas had been distracted by something the way he often was. He could spend minutes staring at the fleshy outline of a morel mushroom or a line of ants marching up a tree. Lina still had some time while Cassie was in a contemplative mood.

"Why do you go up here? Why do you love it so much?"

"I go into the mountains because that is what my family does," Cassie said. "It's what my parents did, and my grandparents before them."

She sat up cross-legged and explained: If your heart was broken, if you were wrestling with a decision, you went high into the places where snow still lingered in August. You left the old miner's trails and went cross country, relying on dead reckoning and gut to get to the secret lakes nobody else knew about, places that didn't even show up on maps. You followed rivers to the places where they began as tiny bubbling springs. You found the early flowers: penstemon, balsamroot, mariposa lily, and the late ones, the hangers-on: paintbrush, shooting star. If you stayed long enough up there, you could even feel the seasons change; the deceptive calm of summer giving way to the frosts of early August.

Everything could be solved in the mountains, if you spent enough time up there, Cassie went on. The trick was to stay long enough to let the mountains get deep into your bones. Most people didn't, Cassie said. Most people ended up longing for what they had left behind: showers, beds, noise to fill up the silence they feared. Most people only had a passing acquaintance with the wild, a handshake, a nod.

"But not me," Cassie said. "Silas and me, we belong up here. That's why I don't go to school. There's nothing I need to know that I can't learn up here."

The storm hit them with an enormous clap of thunder, as if it had been waiting too long for them to make up their minds, and they ran down the mountain laughing, their clothes soaked, their wet hair slapping their faces. Lina had never been so happy.

Thirteen

"**L**et's stay up on the Floor tonight," Cassie said. "We'll bring sleeping bags and popcorn and watch the stars fall from the sky."

Staying out all night? Lina felt anxious at the thought. It was one thing to be gone all day; her mother didn't seem to notice if she was around or not, and Rainy was somewhere down the hill with Danny and the band kids. But at night, they closed themselves up in the house. Nobody left. "I don't think I can."

"Just sneak out. Nobody will know if you're quiet enough."

"She'll hear me. They'll both hear me."

"Don't you know how to do anything? You put the weight on your toes first, then your heels. Breathe between each step. If someone hears you, you're just going to the bathroom. Come on, Tag. It'll be glorious."

❖ ❖ ❖

That night, a shower of pebbles pelted the window. Lina heard the call of an owl.

"Who's out there?" Rainy hissed. She closed her diary and peered out the window into the darkness. "It's that Cassie Van

Allen, isn't it? I know you've still been hanging around with her. Don't you know what people say about her?"

"She's my friend," Lina snapped. "A better friend than you are."

"I hate you." Rainy turned her back, hurt in her eyes, brushing her hair with angry strokes.

Lina ignored her, tiptoeing down the stairs and out into the coolness of the night. She had stashed a bag and a flashlight outside just in case she was brave enough to go.

"I knew it. This looks like a pretty fancy place," Cassie said. She was a dark blur in the night. "I bet you have your own bathroom and everything. Don't tell me. I can guess."

She paced on the gravel, smoke wreathing her head. "I knew you were special, but not this special."

"Cassie, stop." Lina knew everything Cassie said was true.

Rainy poked her head out of the upstairs window. "Lina," she hissed. "Tell her to go. Mom is going to wake up."

"And what's your story?" Cassie asked, looking up at Rainy. She tossed the butt end of her joint down and ground it out. "Are you the good twin? Are you going to come with us, Good Twin? You and me and the Evil Twin, we're going to night hike. The moon is full."

"You'd better not go, Lina," Rainy said. "You'll get in trouble."

Lina had to choose. She stared up at her sister's worried face.

"Let's go," Lina said. She turned her back on the house, on Rainy still in the window.

"Keep to the shadows," Cassie said as they crossed into town. "Last thing we need is some busybody wondering why we're out and about." This late, nothing stirred except the lights thrown from the steamy windows of the Rod and Gun.

Periodically, a drunk would stagger out, peer foggily around, and go back in.

"Is Silas coming?"

"No. He doesn't have to come with us every time. Let's just go up, the two of us."

Night in the forest was different than during the day. The beams from their flashlights seemed too small for the darkness. "Turn it off," Cassie said. "Let your feet feel the trail. The light is just a barrier. Your feet know what to do."

Walking blind, Lina could hear Cassie's footsteps, feel her breath. She stumbled over a root and nearly fell, but soon she saw Cassie was right. Her eyes adjusted to the dark and she saw it wasn't really dark at all, just a deep gray. Soon, Cassie said, the moon would rise.

They rolled out their sleeping bags on the wooden slab. It was so quiet that Lina could hear the distant stream, a melodious trickle cutting through the night. As Cassie had predicted, the moon came up over the Chalks, flooding their clearing with light.

"I never sleep," Cassie said. "By the way."

"You must."

"I never do."

"Why not?"

"I just don't want to, so I don't. You can do that, you know. The mind is stronger than the body."

Lina knew this couldn't be true. Nobody could run on no sleep. Even Cassie, who reminded her of one of those wind-up toys she had as a child.

"Don't you have any other friends you bring here?" Lina asked, thinking too late that this sounded cruel. But Cassie just shrugged.

"I don't have any girlfriends," Cassie said. "It's hard for me. Girls just don't get me. They're either scared of me or they talk about me behind my back. I think it's because sometimes I can still feel the lightning inside of me. Like I told you, I think it's trapped in my body and can't get out. It's like I've swallowed it whole."

"That can't be true."

"Seriously, it's in there. Look," she said. "A shooting star."

A flash of light blazed across the entire sky.

"You're supposed to make a wish. Don't tell me what you wished for. Then it won't come true."

Lina couldn't think of a wish bigger than this one, to have the summer go on forever.

"Listen, wolves," Cassie whispered.

First one long howl, joined by several others. Lina could hear the voices of each wolf as they joined the chorus. It was a primeval sound, long and low, and she shrank closer to Cassie.

They sounded near, but Cassie figured they were over the ridge.

"Hunting," she said, "or just howling because they felt like it." They listened to the musical sounds.

"They wouldn't hurt anyone," Cassie added. "They didn't want anything to do with people. If they see you, they'll turn and run in the other direction.

Nothing was spoken for the longest time. Cassie was so quiet that Lina thought she had fallen asleep after all. Then she said, "Do you have someone you like?"

"You mean a boy?"

"Of course, a boy."

Lina thought of all the boys at school. They shouldered their way through the halls, so sure that the space was given up to them just because they were boys. Then there were boys like Tony Ray, who took what he wanted and didn't look back.

"No. Do you?"

"I'm never getting married," Cassie said. "Never going to fall in love. I don't believe in it. I think it's a lie somebody made up." She rolled herself deeper into her bedroll, only her bright hair showing.

Lina heard Cassie's breath, steady and even. Had she fallen asleep? Lina couldn't imagine sleep ... wider awake than she had ever been.

"Cassie?"

"What, Tag?"

"Is it true what they say about you at school?"

"That I threw a girl down the stairs? Hell yes, I did. Broke her arm. I'd do it again. Do you want to know why?"

"I guess so."

"She was spreading rumors about me. She had heard about the court case and she said that I lied and put my uncle in prison for no reason. Everyone thinks I quit school, but really, they tossed me out. Told me I couldn't come back."

Lina sat up. "But what was she saying? What court case? What about you and your uncle?"

Cassie also sat up. "You mean you haven't heard the stories? My uncle, when he lived with us, before my mother left? He used to come in my room the year I was ten."

Lina felt a growing sense of unease. "What do you mean come in your room?"

"He came in," Cassie said slowly, "and pulled back the covers, and pulled up the long T-shirt I wore to bed, and used to touch me. I don't need to spell this out, do I? He used to chew his nails and I would feel the scrape of them against my skin. He did other things, too. Things I don't want to talk about. But I'll tell you something, Tag. It felt like I was wrapped up in vines and couldn't find my way out. Like those dreams when you're screaming but no sound comes out. It went on for three years."

"Where was your mother?"

"Around," she said. "Out a lot in the bar."

"Didn't you tell her?"

"Not for a while. He said it was our secret, and if I told anyone he would have to hurt Silas. I didn't know what he meant, if he liked little boys that way too. I couldn't take that chance. I saved Silas. I saved him."

Cassie stopped, her breathing deep and angry.

"Finally," she continued, "I couldn't keep it inside. I felt like it would bust me open. I swear, Tag, my body felt as big as a balloon, all that hate trapped inside. I went and I told."

"Then what happened?"

"She didn't believe me at first. Her own brother? Said I was making it up. Said I was looking for attention. But I told her to stay home one night, pretend to be asleep. Listen for the creaky floorboard in my room. So she did, and she caught him. He confessed to it, and went to jail.

"I wish you could have seen her in the courtroom. People say a lot of things about her, that she was a drunk, but she was so fierce. I was only thirteen, but I still remember that."

Cassie didn't say anything else for a long time. She had gone away, the way she sometimes did. At those times, Silas had confided to Lina, Cassie was in another place, a place where nobody else could go. It took her, he said, forever to come back.

Lina lay there in the darkness, her eyes wide open. She felt ashamed. All the things she disliked about her own family suddenly seemed superficial. Her absent mother, her wandering father, Rainy finding a new life, were nothing compared to Cassie's family.

Then Cassie said, "He's going get out soon."

"Your uncle? From prison?"

"He's getting out soon, I said, didn't you hear me? You know the first place he'll go? Like a shot, straight here. I'm the one who put him there. I've got to be more careful than ever."

"Can't you tell the police?"

"The police," she said, and laughed. "The police are for people like you."

"That's not true," Lina protested, but knew Cassie was right. The Van Allens were usually on the wrong side of the law, and everyone expected them to fight their own battles.

"What are you going to do?" she asked.

"It could be ages," Cassie answered. "Or it could be tomorrow. No way of knowing. Just keeping a lookout. It's all I can do. Sometimes I feel like he's already here. When we're walking through the woods, I can almost hear him. I can almost see him. But then I turn around and he's not there."

There was no moon, and she could barely see the trees above them. She clicked on her flashlight, and the weak beam bounced across the dark trunks and tall grass.

"Don't worry, Lina," Cassie half laughed, "I don't feel him right now. We're safe tonight."

Lina didn't know how Cassie knew that, but she turned off her light. She lowered her voice just in case someone was listening. "Why did your mother really leave? Was it what you said?"

"Some of it was true. Things just weren't the same after that. My father blamed her for what my uncle did. Said he knew my uncle was no good, should never have taken him in, that marrying her was the biggest mistake of his life. She gave it back as good as he did, said that she had been warned about marrying a Van Allen. That trouble just flocks to them. They fought a lot, not knockdown, drag out ... just words. You know what though, Tag? The words were almost worse. Then one day, she just took off. I remember that she made my lunch for school that day. She even put in Twinkies. She never did that. Said our teeth would rot clean out because we couldn't afford the dentist. But I opened up my lunch bag and there they were. I didn't know that I'd come home, and she'd be gone. It's pretty much been me and Silas ever since then. My father doesn't really count. He was there, but not really there, you know what I mean?"

"Do you know where she is?"

"Nope." Cassie had lit up a joint; she blew a stream of smoke toward the sky. "I keep thinking that maybe she'll just blow back in with the wind like she never left. And then I think, what will I say? Will I be all happy that she's back? Or will I wish she had stayed gone?"

"My father leaves a lot," Lina said. She watched the orange glow move toward Cassie's mouth and away again. "I know what that feeling's like."

"I know you do," Cassie said. "That's one of the reasons I let you hang around that first day. I thought you might get it. In that way, you're in the same boat as me. We have to stick together."

She reached out and captured Lina's palm with hers. Cassie ran warm, her skin always radiating heat, as if the sun had taken up living in her body. On the other hand, Lina was always cold, like the moon. She felt the heat from Cassie's body flow into hers, warming all of the cold places.

"Thanks for being my friend," Cassie whispered so softly Lina could barely hear it. She fell asleep holding Cassie's hand, but when she woke just before dawn, Cassie had moved away, back into her own space.

❖ ❖ ❖

Rainy sat up in bed, taking Lina in—wrinkled, sour-smelling clothes, hair in a messy ponytail.

"Why did you do that?" Rainy snapped. "You just took off ... with Cassie Van Allen!"

"She's not like they say," Lina mumbled. She hated how it was between them now. How could she bring Rainy back to her? She wanted both lives—with Rainy the way it had always been, and the other life, dirty and sweaty on the trails with Cassie and Silas. She didn't want to give up either one.

She thought of long winter nights in their flannel gowns, their voices spiraling through the darkness, the safety in knowing that there was someone just one bed over. It suddenly seemed like too much to lose. Maybe she could keep Rainy close if she let her in on one secret. Not everything. Just one small thing to unite them again.

"They're living on their own in that shop," she said, seeing Rainy's mouth drop open. "No parents. You can't tell anyone. Promise me you won't."

"They're living there? Without their parents? That isn't even allowed. If they knew at school, both of them would be out of here so fast."

Lina felt a stab of fear. This wasn't going the way she expected. She had expected sympathy, promises of secrets kept, advice. But Rainy chattered on as if she hadn't spoken. "That just seals it. You need to stop hanging around with them and be around here more ... at least for Mom. You've seen her, she doesn't even do Jane Fonda workouts anymore. Just sits around with those awful green shakes. There's something wrong with her. She knows it, we know it."

Rainy pushed her covers aside and got up. "Okay? You'll stop seeing them?"

Lina looked past her sister and out the open window, the cool morning air having worked its way inside, smelling of sage and pine.

"I don't know," she mumbled.

"Think about it," Rainy ordered. "And you can't hang around Silas at school. You'll be an outcast same as him. You can't do that to me. I'll never forgive you, swear to God."

❖ ❖ ❖

The threat of school had been building for a long time and now, the first week of September, Lina knew that everything was about to change. Gone would be the warm afternoons, the vanilla smell of ponderosa down low, the fresh sweet lake water they jumped into after working on the trails. Soon, maybe even this month, the snow would start to fall. Lina walked up to the shop and peered in.

"Cassie isn't here," Silas said. He cranked open the door of the pickup they had been working on all summer. "She's out hunting for a rock drill. If she finds one, it'll be so great. No more pounding for hours with the rock bar. The drill will zip through the rocks in minutes."

"Tomorrow's school," Lina said. "We won't be able to work

on the trails anymore."

"Check it out," Silas said, as though he had not heard her. He hopped in the cab and he turned the ignition key. "We did it. It runs."

They had worked on the truck when it rained, or when Cassie was somewhere else, doing whatever Cassie did on those days. They had completely rebuilt the engine. Replaced the brakes. Run fluids through the thirsty body of the truck until it purred. Each time they fixed something, Silas would turn the key and Lina held her breath. There had been only a disappointing click every time.

Silas's smile filled up most of his face. "Hey. When school starts, let's take the truck. Want to ride with me to school?" he asked.

"You aren't even old enough to drive."

"Then you can drive it. You're almost sixteen. You can get a learner's permit. I wouldn't just let anyone drive this truck, but you can."

A thin knife of fear in between her ribs. *I'll never forgive you.* "I need to walk with my sister," Lina said. Her voice sounded as feeble as she felt.

Silas frowned. "No, you don't," he said. "You haven't hung out with her all summer."

"Well, Heartbreak Creek Helen," Lina said. "You know we aren't supposed to go anywhere alone."

"That's crap," Silas said. "You've walked up here alone a thousand times. You aren't scared of Helen. What is it really?"

❖ ❖ ❖

Because of what Rainy had said, Lina could now see it happen. She would be surrounded by a bright pack of girls. They would chatter like parrots about their summers. Kelly had gotten her braces off. Molly had cut her hair. They would turn to her, their eyes inquisitive. Questions would be flung through the air. Did you ever hook up with Tony Ray? He says you did. Molly might say something about seeing her in a car with Cassie. Heads would turn. Cassie? Cassie Van Allen?

It would be inevitable: Silas would appear, walking down the hall toward them. He might be wearing the cotton shirt Lina had given him. His hair would still be cut short. But it wouldn't be enough.

Because he was Silas, he wouldn't see the warning signs. "Hey, Lina," he would say in his gravelly voice. "Want to go sit outside for lunch?"

The girls would erupt into giggles. They would begin to twitter.

"Lina, why is *he* talking to you?"

"Do you like him?"

"Is he your boyfriend?"

Lina would stand there, uncertain. The light would fade from Silas' eyes, just like that, a curtain falling to shut out any brightness.

Lina wanted to believe that she would tell them that Silas was her friend. That she was going to sit with him at lunch, hang out at the smoker's gate. But she knew deep down that she wouldn't be that brave. Summer was one thing, school another. Instead, she knew she would look away, mumble something cruel. Anything to make Silas go away. She had to protect him, but she didn't know how.

❖ ❖ ❖

"I'll be with my friends," she said miserably to Silas.

He dropped the truck keys with a clatter, swiping at his nose. "I thought you were different!" he yelled. "I thought you were real. You're just like the rest of them."

"No, I'm not! You just don't get it."

"What I get is that you're ashamed of being my friend. You know what? You're worse than they are. At least they say it to my face." He marched over to the door and held it open. "Go home, Lina. Go home where you belong. Cassie was right. You've never belonged here."

As Lina ran down Nip and Tuck, her vision blurred with tears, a flatbed truck passed her, headed up the road. The driver swerved to avoid hitting her. "Get out of the damn road, little girl," a man's voice hollered. Lina stumbled into the ditch where Heartbreak Creek Helen had been found. Like the creek, her own heart felt like it was breaking.

At the house, Rainy was upstairs, ironing her band uniform. "Aren't you going to go to the parade?" she asked. "Everyone goes to the parade."

Lina stood watching the slow, methodic movement of the iron, smoothing out the fabric to something perfect. Finally, her sister stopped and set the iron down. Puffs of steam burst from the hot surface.

"What?" Rainy said. "I have to get this done. Mr. Cane will have a cow if we show up wrinkled."

"Rainy, what would you do if you did something bad? Something that hurt someone?"

"What did you do? Rainy questioned, attacking the purple and yellow uniform with more force than necessary.

"It looks good," Lina said. "You'll look pretty."

Rainy gave her a small smile. She set the iron down again.

"Listen, Lina, if this is about the Van Allens, it's all going to be all right. You don't need to worry about them anymore."

"What do you mean? Rainy! What did you do?"

"Nothing that concerns you. You'll thank me later." Her sister's face set in the obstinate lines that Lina knew well. There wasn't any time to keep asking. She had been wrong to leave the shop. She had to get to Silas and Cassie somehow. It felt urgent, as though nothing else mattered in the world.

Downstairs, her mother looked up from the table where she was mixing her latest potion. Her face looked pale. "Don't go out tonight," she said. "I have a bad feeling about tonight." She had lost weight, a lot of it, Lina saw. Her shoulder blades jutting out of her back like wings, her neck perched on bones, her mother looked like nothing more than a hawk about to take flight. When had that happened? When had she stopped noticing?

Lina stood on one foot and then the other, wanting both to stay and to go. But there would be plenty of time with her mother, later, she told herself. In the winter, when time slowed down, the nights lasting forever. She would stay home then. "I'll be right back," she said. "I promise."

Lina flew out the door. She would fix everything. She ran up Nip and Tuck faster than she had ever run, her feet barely touching the ground. She couldn't wait to get there.

❖ ❖ ❖

"You can't come in here. Not tonight," Silas said. "Not anymore. Not ever, probably." He crossed his arms, letting only a slice of light escape from the room behind him.

Lina tried to peer around him but he blocked her view.

"I didn't mean it, what I said before. I came to say I was sorry." He glared at her. "You need to go away. You can't be up here."

The smell of bleach wafted out underneath the partially closed door. They were cleaning the shop. They did that sometimes, when the grime from the cars Silas fixed got too much. They threw themselves into a frenzy with mops and water and steaming towels until the entire shop gleamed.

"We're leaving tonight," Silas said when Lina didn't move. "I'm just packing up our stuff. The truck runs, me and Cassie are going to take off after dark."

"Leaving? But why?"

Silas hesitated and seemed to choose his words carefully. "Lady from social services came up here today. Knocking on the door, hollering. We pretended we weren't here, locked the door, but she knew. Said through the door that someone had told her there were minors living up here on our own. Now who would have told them that, Lina?"

From far below she heard the parade begin, a revving of the engines that held the floats, the windup of the band. She was aware of Silas' angry face and a sinking sensation in her stomach. Rainy had told.

"Where's Cassie?" she managed, her throat thick with fear.

Silas ran a hand through his hair. "Gone into the woods. She's the worst I've ever seen her. Bolted right out of here, I couldn't even understand what she was saying. She's gone to the Floor, I bet. You should go home. This is just between me and her now."

❖ ❖ ❖

All week the valley had been locked in unusual heat, the river dropping enough that rafts scraped the rocks beneath. Even the nights brought no relief. Something had to break and soon. Each afternoon as Lina worked on the trails, she had watched the top-heavy clouds towering thousands of feet into the sky. Each day she thought that they would surely break open and give them the needed rain. Each day had slipped into night without any change.

She could feel the hushed forest as she climbed upward on the ghost trail. It felt as though the trees were waiting for something the same way she was, as if one touch would cause the world to break open. Though it was evening, and the sun would set soon, it was as hot as noon.

When Lina burst into the clearing, Cassie was standing on the wooden foundation. For a moment it looked as though her hands were on fire. Then she realized that Cassie was flicking lit matches off the Floor and into the air. Most of them went out as they flew, but Lina saw one land in a bed of dry pine needles and start to smolder.

Cassie looked up and saw her. Her face was streaked with something that looked like dirt and tears. "I should have known you'd find me, Tag. You're my little shadow, aren't you? Don't you get tired of following me? Don't stop me. Don't you dare stop me."

"Cassie, what are you doing?" Lina cried. She ran over to the small flame and stamped it under her feet. She could feel the heat through the soles of her boots. Cassie's mother's boots. Hers now.

Cassie had two boxes of matches and she kept lighting them, one by one. Smoke began to rise in small puffs from the deep bed of pine needles around her feet. Still small enough, Lina thought. She could still fix this.

"I'm sorry I told," she cried. "We can fix this."

"What are you going to do, Lina?" Cassie sneered. "Is your mom going to adopt us? Are we going to live in your fancy house with you?" She thrust out her chin. "No? Didn't think so. You know what I'm going to do? I'm going to light this mountain on fire, and you'd better get out of here unless you want to go with it. I mean it."

Smoke curled up between them, momentarily blurring Cassie's face. Lina coughed as it stung her lungs.

"Remember what you said, Cassie? You know, the night we slept up here? Tomorrow is always better?"

"Don't even say it," she said. A match burned perilously close to her fingers. She didn't seem to notice. "Tomorrow takes too long."

Far below her, the parade moved on. If she tried hard enough Lina thought she could hear the high school band cranking up *America the Beautiful.* Rainy would be with them. Little kids would be running for the candy the firemen threw from their truck. Molly and Kelly and all of the others would be there too, pretending to make fun of the unstable floats and the cheerleaders perched on the mayor's 1968 Mustang. Everything down there would be blessedly normal … she had never known how much she wanted to be normal until now.

"Don't you see how everything's changing?" Cassie asked. Her voice was light, conversational. She stared down at the matches in her hand. "Nobody wants to see it. But these trees are dying and I don't know why. Is it because it doesn't snow as much anymore? And the wolves, if they dare show their faces down in the valley, they get poisoned, shot. Why not burn it all now, start over."

Lina shook her head, not understanding. A wave of heat passed between them. She could hear the crackle and spit of flames but didn't dare take her eyes off of Cassie. The air felt charged with danger, as if it would split wide open. Like lighting about to strike, though the sky was bland and cloudless.

"Well?" Cassie said. "Don't you want to try it? Here." She threw a box of matches underhand toward Lina, and she caught it without thinking. "You can't believe how good it feels. Go ahead. Light one."

Still small enough to stamp out, Lina thought. Not big enough to be seen from town, this slow curl of smoke that wreathed upward, not yet touching the afternoon sky. This felt like another test. Would she do what Cassie asked? Follow her as she had done all summer, a tagalong?

Shakily, she scratched the match across the box. She would just light this one and then blow it out, show Cassie she could do it. Then they would stop. They would stomp out the tiny fires and hike back down the ghost trails and into their real lives. But her fingers were sweaty, and the lit match dropped and fell at her feet.

From somewhere that felt far away, Cassie laughed. "I knew you could do it," she said.

Cassie was throwing the matches far enough that they landed beyond where Lina stood. The bright sparks flew through the air as if they loved the sky and wanted to get close to it. "Light some more," Cassie said. "Let's see how brave you really are."

Lina shuffled her feet over the fire she had started, smothering it. She could feel it struggling to live.

"You need to stop, Cassie."

Her hand to her mouth, Lina watched as slowly, almost casually, the fire moved toward a grouping of heavy-boughed trees. Suddenly, it was too big to stop.

Cassie didn't seem to notice that the fire she had lit was backing around behind her; that she was almost surrounded by flame. She had stepped off the Floor and was advancing toward where Lina stood, frozen in place. "You'll be like the rest of them. Out of here in a few years. Yellow River in your rearview. I'll be in some foster home, Silas in another."

"No, Cassie," Lina screamed over the wind. Where had the wind come from? It had been a calm day until now. Had the fire created the wind that tossed the trees around that they swayed and almost touched the ground? Her hair blew into her eyes, her mouth. It was getting harder to breathe as the smoke blew around them, blotting out the air, the sky, everything.

"We'll tell the truth," Lina said. She had to get Cassie out of here, had to find the words that would take the blank stare out of her friend's eyes. She fought to keep her voice steady. "It was an accident! You didn't mean to do it."

She shook her head, her hair wild around her face. "Get out of here, Tag. I mean it."

"It was a mistake! How could you have known it would burn? We'll just tell the truth," Lina cried. But of course, they could have known. They had lived through the summer, pushed our feet through pine needles that broke cleanly in two. Cassie knew how dry it was. She knew that a match, landing in the right place, would start a fire that would not stop.

Fire began to lick at the taller trees on the edge of the clearing. It was moving away from them, downslope, pushed by a steady wind, sweeping in a bright orange arc toward town. It was cutting them off from the trail.

Lina turned to Cassie, who had stopped throwing matches and was watching the fire.

"We can make a run for it," Lina said. "There're other trails going out of here. We'll take one of them and run down to the forest road. We can leave town tonight. We never need to come back. We'll just disappear."

"Tag, you can't disappear. They'll look for you. You're that kind of girl. And me? Nobody's heart would break if I left. You have to get down the mountain right now, before it's too late."

Lina knew Cassie was right. She had to make a choice.

Cassie's face was drained of color, her voice choked to a harsh whisper from the smoke. "You have to find Silas before anyone else does. Tell him to get out of town by himself. Don't come back, not ever. Make him promise."

"Cassie, wait. You need to come with me. I don't know the way!"

Lina had heard that sometimes animals would run into a fire rather than away from it. It was as though the sudden heat confused them. The heart of the fire beckoned to them the same way moths were drawn to light ... irresistible.

Cassie ran into the fire rather than away from it, even though Lina tried to stop her. She reached for her, grabbed her long dark coat, clumps of her curly hair, but she slipped through Lina's grasp, eluding her. The last Lina saw of her, Cassie was outlined in flame, a girl surrounded by fire. Then she disappeared. She dove into the fire as though it were water.

❖ ❖ ❖

That was the story Lina had always believed to be true, but there was one small thing she had forgotten, the moment when she almost saved Cassie.

It went like this: Cassie had turned away from her, climbed back up on the Floor, and stepped to the edge as if she were going to jump.

"Cassie," Lina screamed. She grabbed at Cassie, but her fingers only pulled on her jacket. There was a moment when Lina felt Cassie's body fall back against hers, but one of the small fires she had set suddenly caught a larger tree. It roared up the branches and climbed to the top. The tree exploded and Lina screamed. In that moment she lost her grip. Her face flushed like sunburn, Lina turned and ran. Because of Cassie, because of what Cassie had shown Lina, she knew there was another ghost trail leading her away from the fire. She climbed, lungs on fire, and found it, a path that had been built all wrong, on the fall line. Someday, Cassie had said, someday we will fix it. Lina ran down it, faster than she had ever run. At one point, far below, she looked back up. Smoke was starting to billow from beneath the trees. As she watched, a tree exploded and the fire rolled down the mountain like an avalanche, pushed by the downslope wind. It also moved uphill; past all the places she knew and had yet to know.

It seemed that she ran forever, stumbling over the rocks and the downed trees, until she came out to the road's end. Then she walked toward the red and blue lights.

Fourteen

Even though she knew better, Lina had imagined that nothing would have changed. She and Silas would climb up the old trail, obscured now by fire-weakened trees and new brush, but because they knew it, because the knowledge of it was stuck in their bones, they would find clues to where the old cabin had been. They would follow the ridge up toward the sky to the place they called the Floor. Lina thought that the cabin might still be there, somehow spared from the fire, a wooden platform built with sweat and dreams, a place where deer slept under in summer, their hearts close to the cool dirt. Lina and Silas would lie on their backs the way they used to, whole hours passing without saying a word. Maybe, if they were lucky, they would hear the distant howl of wolves.

Somehow, Lina thought, they would be able to bridge the gap between who they were now and who they had been. Silas would tell her what secrets Cassie had kept, what had driven her up the mountain that night. Lina would open all the parts of her that were clenched like a fist. Her life would roll out in front of her, free of fear and regret.

❖ ❖ ❖

They drove to the shop. It was a house now, entirely different on the inside. The former cement floor was now covered with honey-colored hardwood. Silas had cut a window in the frame so there was a view of the Chalks. He had roughed in a kitchen and placed a clawfoot tub in the bathroom. A bed was separated from the rest of the room by a half wall.

"Did most of this myself," he said. "It's nothing like those summer houses, but this is all I need."

The place bore no resemblance to the cold shop where he and Cassie had lived, a pair of feral children in ragged clothes, a pile of stolen tools in the corner, carefully rationed food in a rubber tote. This was a place that someone could call home, a refuge.

Lina and Silas went light, with only what they needed. A couple of sandwiches, a bottle of wine, sleeping bags and coats. They didn't need much more in early September. But they needed to move; the light would fade in a couple of hours.

Walking with their packs, they had almost stepped off from the end of the road into the wilderness when Silas turned to look back. It was something Cassie had always done, as if to see if anyone was watching. This time, someone was.

"Well look here," Silas said. "We have us a convoy."

Two familiar pickups barreled up the road.

Her father's truck led the way, lurching up and grounding to a halt. It had turned over three hundred thousand miles and unless he put some time into it, it wouldn't last much longer. But he was like that, ignoring the problem, believing everything would work out for the best. It needed so much, a complete engine rebuild, but Lina knew he would never take the time for that. Instead, the truck would sputter to a painful death on some back road, him staring puzzled out the windshield with a sense of betrayal.

"What are you doing here?" Lina couldn't keep the irritation from her voice.

His grin faltered a little. "That's not much of a welcome, Tazlina. Cherry Creek was a bust. Took some wind out of my sails. Nothing out there but cows and poison ivy and a shit ton of rattlesnakes. Went back through the Imnaha but you were gone, not at that shop. Ran into Joe in the tavern. Thought we should join forces, come check to see if you were all right."

Joe Grider got out from the second pickup and came over to sling an arm around Lina's waist.

"Well, butter my butt and call me a biscuit, Dane. We've done tracked her down."

"Sure did. Anytime you want to go out hunting with me, give me the word."

"Nah," Joe said. "I'm more about peace these days. Peace and a bit of fly fishing." He scuffed his boot in the hard-packed dirt and fixed her with a hard stare. "You OK, Taz? For real?"

When she nodded, her father barreled on. "Tazlina, I went by the cabin to see if you were there. Still standing, isn't it? One of these days I think I'll let the Forest Service have it. They've been after it for years. Only they'd bulldoze it all, landscape it, try to make it look natural. Erase all signs that we ever lived there."

Lina imagined their old house collapsing in on itself like a long sigh. Maybe that would be better, she thought. Nobody had wanted them there in the first place.

"McCarthys always land on their feet," he continued. "Tougher than the rest by a long shot." He slapped his hat on his jeans, releasing a cloud of dust. "Silas, you're a local. Any bright ideas where I might uncover some treasure?" Back in the day, we shared our leads. We worked together. Not all these lone wolves."

Silas had been hovering on the outskirts of the conversation. Now he stepped forward, dropping his backpack on the ground. "Have you ever been in the Warbonnet drainage?" he asked. "That's as wild as it gets in the Chalks. No trails, just a whole lot of remote country. Lakes. Waterfalls. Seems like a good place to hide something."

"You know what? I've seen that on the map," Dane said. "I like the way you think. I've got some provisions ... I could spend a week prowling around in there. Thanks for the tip, son."

Dane turned to Joe, slapping him on the shoulder. "Take care of my girl."

"You got it," Joe said, "if she'll let me."

Dane turned to Lina. He shook his head with a wry grin. "You always land on your feet, Tazlina. Proud of you for that. See you next time."

Her father catapulted himself into the pickup with the agility of a younger man. Rolling down the window, he shouted, "I'll be back in a week, maybe two. I'll hunt you down again, let you know how it went." Mashing the accelerator, he tore down the road. Her father, leaving again. In spite of herself, Lina felt a smile curve her lips. He would never change.

Joe cleared his throat. "So, who is this?" he asked, indicating Silas. "Going to introduce us?"

The two men sized each other up. Joe spoke first. "I'm Joe Grider, range rider, ranch hand, all around ne'er do well. Pleased to meet you."

"Silas Van Allen. Been here forever." And you haven't, Lina could tell he wanted to add.

"Listen," Joe said, "if you don't mind? I need a word with Taz here. I drove seven hours to find her. Alone," he added with an edge to his voice.

For a moment Lina thought Silas wasn't going to give up any ground, but finally he nodded and walked a few paces away, watching Joe carefully.

"Who told you where I was?" she asked.

Joe nodded. "Lucy ... she has kin everywhere. Probably has folks who got burnt out of this valley. Told me she recognized your name when you moved there. Knew you would be heading back here someday for some kind of reckoning."

All those gifts from the garden, the friendly waves from the road, and Lucy had stayed silent. "But she never said anything to me about it."

He held her chin in his fingers and looked deep into her eyes. "Of course, she didn't. Those Imnaha people, they don't go talking all over town. She only told me because she knew I was worried sick about where you had gone."

Lucy knew the whole time and she hadn't thought any less of Lina. She turned that over in her mind for a minute. But Joe was still speaking in a low growl.

"Now, this guy over here staring us down. He's part of it, isn't he? I don't really like the looks of him. Looks like he'd knife you as soon as look at you."

"He's all right," Lina said. "He used to be my friend. Still is, maybe. He has answers that I need." She looked at Joe, calmly gnawing on a blade of grass. He was not as uncomplicated as she had imagined. "You drove all this way. You must have driven through the night. Did you think I needed saving?"

"You're the last person who needs saving, babe," he said. "Don't you know that? After I saw Lucy, I went into the tavern for some fortification. Dane was in there and he was hunting you up too. Besides, driving like a bat out of hell served me well this time."

"I just need a little more time," Lina said. "Then I'll be done." Her words sounded hollow, but Joe seemed to believe her.

"Listen," he said. "Put the past to rest and come on home. I don't judge you or anyone. Whatever happened up here, it's over and done. Ain't nobody going to change it now."

He fumbled for a cigarette and winced. "Forgot, I quit two days ago. Tell you what. Come with me right now. I'm headed to the Great Basin. That's where I was going, but I flipped a U turn. I'd been downriver, thinking a few things over. Missed you. Caught me off guard. Don't recall missing anyone before. Figured that was worth thinking over a bit. Figured you were worth a detour. You'll love it there, Taz, honest."

Waiting for her answer, he reached in the cab and pulled out a Hamms, cracked it open and drank, throwing his head back. "Nothing better than a road soda after a long drive," he said, and laughed. "Some things I can't give up."

Silas was still watching them, and she gestured for him to stay where he was. Joe's face clouded. "Don't want to leave you alone with him. It doesn't sit right that you didn't confide in me about all of this."

Lina hesitated. "I don't confide in anybody. There was a girl I knew once. My friend. She told me to keep a poker face … don't let them know how you really feel. I took that to heart."

"That probably served you pretty well back then," Joe said. "Now? Different story. Friends are all we have. Can't go it alone forever." He crushed the beer can with his boot and threw it back in the pickup. "Don't take too long. I'll be down on the Alvord, waiting for you."

He leaned down and kissed her short and sweet, the way

he always did. He nodded once in farewell and swung into his truck. Gunning it, he was gone in seconds.

"Who the hell was that?" Silas said. "He's a force of nature, isn't he? Imagine driving over the Snake on a whim and a prayer." Silas looked wistful, as if he wished he were that kind of man. "What is he to you?"

"He brought me firewood the first winter," she said, remembering. "Larch wood, the very best kind, when nobody else could get it. That's how we met, he heard someone was living up there and showed up with a cord and a half."

"That's not what I asked, Lina. Is he your boyfriend, husband?"

She felt her face flush.

"Not sure," she stammered. "He tells me stories that don't quite match up. Then he disappears for weeks on end, shows up when I least expect it. That's Joe in a nutshell."

Somehow Joe had picked her out of all the other women in the Imnaha Canyon, women who were handy with a horse and a gun and a post pounder. She was still not sure why, or what to do about it.

"Sounds like your father," Silas said.

Joe and Dane are nothing alike, Lina began to snap back, but it occurred to her that they sort of were—men who moved through lives like rivers in flood. Men she could spend her whole life trying to pin down.

"Why did you send him to the Warbonnet?" Lina asked. "You know there's nothing there."

Silas shrugged. "Don't know that there's not. Sounds like he really doesn't want to quit, and it's as good a place as any." He slung his pack over his shoulders and drew the hip belt tight. "If we're going, we better do it. Losing daylight. Unless you're expecting someone else? Come on, you go first. You remember your way up here. It hasn't changed that much."

But it had. The ghost trail had nearly vanished with fire and time. The silver trunks of the vanquished and the burn-scarred of the survivors lined the route that they used to take. The brush had seen its chance and had crept in, forcing her to guess at where the trail had once gone. Sometimes Lina caught sight of a tree she had once cut, the chopped ends still protruding, and she could barely make out the outlines of the old switchbacks, climbing steadily through the now bleak forest.

"Look," Silas said. "There's our rock wall."

Lina drew in her breath. The wall was still intact, even the heart still in place. "It lasted. It really lasted." The heart had kept it intact.

"The fire came down through here," Silas said. But Lina could see which way it had gone by the old black scars on the trunks of the surviving trees. Down the fall line, like Cassie had told her. Fire, like water, taking the lazy way.

"They managed to save the buildings at the end of the road, because the fire parted there," Silas said. "It ran on down the hill over sixty miles an hour, burned down some houses, then ran up the side of the Chalks. I was safe because my building didn't burn. I stood there and watched it. The fire went right around the road here. It got pretty hot, but the volunteer fire department was up here hosing everything down. They were outgunned for sure."

Because she was in front and couldn't see his face, it felt safe to ask. "When did you know that Cassie didn't come back down?"

She held a branch so he could duck underneath.

"I kind of always knew," he said. "I thought she went up here. I told her not to, I told her to stay in town. I had a feeling she would have gone, though. I thought maybe the fire was from lightning, but we hadn't had a storm in weeks. I put two and two together pretty quick. And then I saw you," he said. "I saw you come running out of the woods to the sheriff's car."

Lina stopped so abruptly that he stumbled into her. "You saw me? Why didn't you come over?"

"Us Van Allens and the law, we don't have a good relationship," he said. "The last thing I wanted to do was have the sheriff poking around in the shop. Asking questions. There was already some social worker after us, someone in town told, I think. I didn't know what you were doing up there and why you came down running like something had spooked you good, but I figured I'd find out soon enough. Only, they sent you away before I could find out. And when I saw you, no Cassie, I told myself that maybe you were looking for her and didn't find her. That maybe Cassie was just somewhere else, who knows where she went sometimes. Sometimes she would just up and disappear for a few hours. But she never came home, not that night and not the night after that. Finally, when the people who took me away showed up, they told me Cassie was never coming back. That my father said he couldn't take care of me, he had too much going on down in Twin. He signed me away. I haven't seen him since."

Rainy told, she almost said. But what did it matter? The end would have been the same.

They had been climbing for what felt like hours, following a path that existed mostly in memory. Trees had fallen, their roots pummeled by fire and snow, forcing Lina and Silas to climb around or over them. Brush had taken over the places where they had cut it back so fiercely. But the outlines remained. Nothing ever truly went away.

"Fire was a mosaic," Silas said, stopping to take a drink of water. "Skipped around this mountain, took what it wanted, left some the way it was. The wind drove it, so it didn't stick around here long."

She moved aside to let him lead the way. A wall of seemingly impenetrable, sharp-toothed brush had closed in, leaving no sign of a path. They had to be close to the Floor, but there was no clear way to go. This seemed like the end.

"We built a climbing turn here," Silas said. He shouldered through the brush, forcing a path to the other side. "Come through here. You can find the trail if you look. See the old cut log here? The place where we put a blaze on that tree? It's here, you just have to look closer."

Lina chose to trust Silas and followed through a spiky tunnel, sharp thorns scraping across her skin, pulling at her hair. She stumbled free into the open.

"Here it is," Silas said.

They were at the place where the old cabin floor had been. The fire had cleared away the small trees that had been taking over the meadow, and the sun shone on a carpet of grass. There was a view now too, the same view the people who had started to build the cabin had chosen, but which had grown obscured as the big trees filled in the gaps. Some of those trees were gone now, leaving empty spaces where they could stand and look out over the valley far below.

"It's beautiful up here now, so open," Lina said. Behind her, Silas had been poking around in a tangle of logs.

"Lina, it's still here. The Floor is still here."

He was right. Somehow the fire had spared the wood foundation, maybe because it had spread downhill first, pushed by the evening wind, the same wind that had blown the flames into town. A lodgepole pine had fallen across the far end, but they could still sit on the wooden slab the way they had so long ago.

"I can't believe it survived. Fire does strange things," Silas said. "Maybe one day, I'll come up and finish this cabin. Stay up here and never come down." He shook his head. "Probably not."

They watched the distant valley in silence.

"Lina, I want to know everything about where you went," he suddenly said. "Where they took you. Maybe if I hear it, I can begin to understand why you did what you did."

"Silas," Lina said. "I tried to save her. I was afraid. The fire was all around us."

"You were always afraid!" It came out as a shout. "Until we took you in, you were scared of everything. Rivers. The Staircase. Of being who you were, instead of who you thought you should be. And honestly, Lina? I don't see that you've changed at all. So what good was it? Should we have turned you away, that first day? Would it have been better if we had never known you at all?"

"No," she said softly, almost too softly for him to hear, she thought. "It was the best thing that ever happened to me. You and Cassie, the best thing."

What had the clerk called him? Weird? Strange? She could see how others would think that. Silas seemed to swing from high to low, just like the capricious summer thunderstorms on the peaks. There were no clues on how to prepare, because you didn't see the complicated play of air and water until they combined in towering clouds. Something boiled deep in Silas, and it didn't take much for it to come to the surface.

"Tell me, then," he said, his voice holding an edge. "Tell me where you went ... after. We've got all night."

There was so much that she wanted to tell him, but it was the younger Silas she wanted to speak to, the outcast kid with his heart too open, a sprinkle of freckles like pepper across his angular face. That kid would understand.

How could she explain the storm inside a teenage girl, that stew of desire and fear that rolled around in her belly at fifteen?

"I wanted it all," she said slowly, realizing that this was the truth. "My sister, the way it used to be with us. Being part of Molly's group, and to have you and Cassie as my friends, all at the same time. I didn't know how to choose just one. That was my mistake, thinking I could have everything."

She looked over at him, steeling herself for what she was about to say.

"Silas, let me tell you what happened."

Fifteen

Lina's father stood at their door with folded arms and a grim expression. He had come home at last, summoned not by love but duty.

"Get your things," he said abruptly as the sheriff approached.

By then, it was a week into the fire, long enough for the initial panic to subside. Many of the townspeople were still sheltered in the high school, their minds numb, their homes no longer standing, their lives shattered.

It had not taken long for the first fire crews to respond. Eventually, crews would arrive from all over the country. This was the Big One, a catastrophic fire that everyone had worried about for years, watching the slow march of pine beetles across the mountain. The only difference was that they had expected the danger to come from lightning, not a girl with a match.

And still the mountain grumbled with fire, the drumbeat of helicopter rotors filling the valley from dawn until dusk. Some places still burned so hot that even the fire crews had backed off. Trees could fall without warning, their roots so damaged that there was nothing to hold them upright. The entire Isolations were engulfed, and the fire had jumped the river and the highway and was encroaching into the Chalks.

Backpackers had to be lifted out by helicopter. With no rain in sight, maybe the cold of late fall or the freeze of winter would put it out. Maybe. Fires overwintered sometimes, hiding in stumps, waiting out the snow.

Lina sat silent as her father and the sheriff discussed logistics and her fate. Her life was spinning out of control and there was no way to stop it. It was as though she were deep underwater, voices muffled, faces out of focus. Her father had described being caught under a rapid before it spit him out, a dizzying tumble through indifferent water. At the time, she and Rainy had rolled eyes at each other: the same old stories, as if Dane were desperate to let them know he had once been truly alive. Now she could imagine how it must have been.

The sheriff, who looked as though he had not slept in days, took a step toward Lina.

"Good thing most everyone was at the parade," he said sharply. "No time for evacuation orders, people just looked up and saw the fire coming, most couldn't make it back to their houses. The ones that did just had time to grab a few things and go. Else, we would have had deaths on our hands." *On your hands*, he didn't say.

The sheriff turned back to her father.

"Your daughter's case was fast tracked," he said, "on account of the fire and how people felt about her. At this point, I can't be responsible for her safety. There's a deputy outside waiting to get her out of here tonight. There's an open spot waiting for her."

The wilderness therapy program, he said, was a good place to put teenagers like Lina, who needed to be straightened out.

"Three years," the sheriff said, as though that were inconsequential. "After that, most of the girls in the program will go on to a residential boarding school, where they can buckle down and get their diplomas away from distractions." He looked again at Lina. "Then there might be help with college if she applies herself. Scholarships. Assistance. It's up to her."

❖ ❖ ❖

They called it wilderness therapy, as if a person could speak to the wild in the land and it would talk back. As if Lina could have a conversation with the stark black night skies and the sandstone arches and the thirsty creosote bush. And sometimes, she felt she could: like she was less of flesh and blood and more of the earth. There were days when she saw nobody else but the other girls and it seemed like they were being absorbed by the desert, as she were turning into it herself, her skin stained red from the dust, her limbs becoming as tough as tree branches.

They spent months crossing desert washes and camping in among rabbitbrush and creosote. When they found water, it was a gift and one they knew to conserve. They strained it through bandannas, one precious drop at a time. Most of the time their camps were dry, backpacks loaded down with several liters of water, their hair going gritty with fine sand. They were feral girls, and after thirty days none of them could imagine anything else.

The desert was as different from the mountains as the moon. With fifteen other girls, Lina walked for weeks with a backpack, searching for water. The instructors handed her a map and compass, showing her where to find the natural seeps, where water was rumored to ooze out of rocks and drip slowly into their bottles. She learned to identify the bright blue life-giving lines on the map, the dashed ones that meant an ephemeral stream, the bold ones that meant surely water was perennial. She matched map to country, following dry canyons to where the secret water hid.

During long rainless days, Lina walked through a maze of red rocks formed by long-gone rivers, towers of stone higher than her head. Everywhere was the reminder of where water had once been. Sometimes the skies opened up and water would appear everywhere, flowing down the pour-offs, filling up the sandy canyon bottoms in flash flood. Just as quickly as the water had come, it would vanish, leaving only pockets of wet dirt and potholes in the rocks.

They walked down sloping slickrock, Lina's feet sticking to the smooth surface, diving down into deeply incised canyons. After a time, it seemed as though they were the only girls on the planet, the only ones who mattered.

With the falling of the sun, the face of the desert was different than in the mountains. A skeleton moon pierced the soft darkness. Small creatures rustled the robe of the night. Girls who had been silent for years began to talk, unraveling themselves and the cords that had bound them tight.

"You're here because you have lost your way," the instructors—Heidi and Sam—told them. They had to find our own route, like the maps they carried. It would be as difficult as finding water, they said. It could take them years.

Heidi and Sam were only five years older than Lina was, but they seemed decades ahead of her. They knew how to start fires with bow drills, and how to strip a succulent plant for water if they desperately needed it. They were not afraid of the dark. They had once been in the program, they said, and their lives had been turned around. Hers would too.

Once they went out with flashlights to find the secretive desert night lizard. Worth finding, the lizards changed color depending on the light, from a deep tan to almost black. Somehow, they sensed the right color to be camouflaged.

After they had trudged, sleep-deprived and cranky, for the several miles that Heidi insisted they hike, the girls huddled in a circle in the deep desert night. Lina's lips were gritty with the taste of sand, she longed for sleep, and they never found one single lizard.

"You can just blend in and take the colors of others all your life," Heidi said. "But it's better to figure out who you're going to be on your own."

Lina rolled her eyes at Misty, the girl assigned to be her camp buddy, and Misty rolled hers back. Heidi and Sam turned everything into a teaching moment.

"What's so bad about not blending in?" Lina whispered to Misty as they stumbled back to camp. She thought about Cassie and Silas and how they hadn't seemed to care how much they stuck out. Lina had believed they held some secret but look at what had happened to them.

"Are you crazy?" Misty asked. She peeled back the wrapper of a Snickers, gone liquid in the hot desert air. "I'd give anything to blend in."

They went back to their sleeping bags and Lina lay awake for a long time, hearing Misty's impatient breath beside her. Misty always tossed and turned, fighting sleep as much as she fought everything in life. "Lina?" she whispered finally.

Lina peered over at the lumpy shapes of other sleeping bodies. Nobody moved. "What is it?"

"Don't you wish that we could stay out here for good? This is the only place I've ever felt normal."

On their wilderness solo, where all the girls had to hike to spots that Heidi had identified and stay there with a jug of water, a sleeping bag, and a journal for twenty-four hours, Misty was the only one who didn't come back into camp relieved to be done. Instead, she told Lina, she had thought about taking a runner, just disappearing into the desert for good.

"Why didn't you?" Lina asked. Somewhere out there, there had to be a road that people drove, a way to get to somewhere else. Girls escaped sometimes, tracked down days or weeks later, sent to someplace worse than this.

Misty turned onto her back, her sleeping pad rustling in protest. "I know you said your mom's sick, your sister's moving away. But at least you've got people. If I ran, where would I go? I like it out here. Like I said, it's the first time I've ever felt normal." She shifted on the pad again. Next to them, someone snored softly. "You know something, Lina? Normal is underrated. There's nothing wrong with normal."

Cassie had told her that the wilderness could heal, but now Lina saw it. The other girls opened like ripe flowers. She could see their outer skins falling away with every day they spent out there. By the end, all of them were raw and new. They were different girls than they had been before, girls without shells. To the outside world, they would still seem tough, not easily bruised, but when they were all together, where it was safe, their eyes shone with easy tears, they hugged and laughed easily.

By the end of her time in the desert, the winter was upon them, the landscape stark and frozen ... without warmth. Each day seemed the same: packing up her sleeping bag and tent with frozen fingers, hiking ten to fifteen miles from one nameless ridge to another, punctuated by snack breaks and stops for discussions that always had a moral lesson. Though all the girls complained, Lina knew that this was where she was supposed to be. She couldn't imagine being tossed out into the "real" world like a piece of driftwood, to survive on her own. How would that even work?

Girls came back sometimes, to work as instructors. They brought stories of how hard they had tried in society. It was cruel out there, they said, all billable hours and long commutes and men at the higher positions wanting them to fail. These stories terrified Lina. Better to stay here, in the wilderness, where everyone was sort of equal.

One afternoon, the group was hiking at the bottom of Oregon, having moved through Nevada before they were to loop back again. Purposely, Lina and Misty veered off the trail to pee. Sometimes neither of them needed to go, but this was the only time they weren't watched.

Quite by accident, they stumbled upon a hidden hot spring. The whole valley they had walked through had springs like this, but most were off limits, way too hot. The water, if they were to jump in, would peel off their skin, the instructors had warned. People had died that way. The earth's crust was just a thin membrane here, covering the boiling magma below.

But this spring was different. A trickle of cool water from a stream above transformed it into a steamy pool surrounded by river rock. Lina peeled off her clothes and sank chin-deep in the hot water, Misty following. They knew it was risky ... they could get in trouble, lose privileges, but Lina didn't care. The rest of her life seemed like distant fog, too far away to consider.

Besides, most of the other girls lagged behind, some of them plodding only a mile an hour, with Sam the sweep. The girls up front at Heidi's heels had something to prove or the need to burn more calories. Lina and Misty were in the middle, the coveted position where they were unobserved by staff. Lina knew it could be hours before the slow group reached them; they would proclaim defeat or blisters several times, delaying their arrival.

"Where are you going to go when you get out?" Misty asked as she leaned back against the rock, closing her eyes. She had kept on her tank top and underwear; she never let anyone see her entire body.

"To school, dork. Aren't you? We have to finish high school."

"I know," she said. "I mean, after that. Where do you think you'll go?"

What anyone was going to do, after, was a favorite topic of conversation among all of them. They could spend hours at it, interrupted only by Heidi or Sam, who would gently chide them, telling them that the only time that was important was now. They would roll their eyes once more and wait until the instructors ventured out of earshot to pick up the discussion again. Other than Misty, none of them wanted to live in the present and the past would break their hearts. The future was the only safe place.

Some of the girls dreamed big while others dreamed small. Joann said she was moving to Paris, to live in a garret and be a starving artist. Selena said the Caribbean was more her style. A hammock and an umbrella drink were all she needed. A few of the others just wanted to go back to their hometowns and slip back into the lives they had been forced to abandon. Sitting cross-legged in a dry desert wash, they planned out our lives in minute detail: the crusty bread that they would buy every day from the bakery, the herbs they would grow in planters on their windowsills, the mysterious men with foreign accents whom they would string along.

Lina had no idea. She was afraid of the future, looming closer each day like a thunderhead on the horizon. She couldn't go back to Yellow River Valley ... she wouldn't be safe. Plus, Rainy and their mother, hiding tears and anger, had packed up all their belongings and left forever.

"What about that kid, Silas?" Misty asked. "Could you try to find him?"

"I wouldn't even know where to start," Lina said. She told Misty what she knew, what Rainy had told her: Silas had vanished like a rock thrown in water, the shop abandoned. He could be anywhere.

"I know a place," Misty said. "My brother told me about it. Want to hear?"

Lina knew that two years before, Misty's brother had vanished too, leaving their family either by accident or design. He had been wandering the country, trying to find himself, Misty had said. He sent them postcards from Yellowstone, Devils Tower, Glacier National Park. Then one day the postcards stopped coming.

"One of the postcards was of a place called Hells Canyon," Misty said. "There's a river at the bottom, and that's the border between Idaho and Oregon. My brother wrote that if you wanted to get away, this was the place to do it. He said the canyon is five thousand feet deep from rim to river. I always kind of thought I'd like to see it someday."

In the distance Lina saw approaching flashlights, their beams bouncing off the desert scrub. "Oh man, busted again," Misty said. She heaved herself out of the pool in an explosion of water. "Hey, Lina. If we ever get out of here alive, let's take a road trip up there, to Hells Canyon."

It would never happen.

Twelve days before they were set to be released, Misty cut herself so deeply in the bathroom of a gas station that blood ran like rivers down the walls. Surely it was an accident, the devastated instructors cried. said. They knew that none of the girls were supposed to be left alone, anytime, anywhere. They had gotten lax in the last month, trusting them. But it wasn't an accident. Lina knew Misty, the abundant body she despised, the despair that she hid behind the pranks she pulled at camp. Everything Misty did was for a reason.

❖ ❖ ❖

After the desert, Lina was sent to a residential boarding school, nicknamed the Bad Place. It was easier. There were plenty of places to hide, even in plain sight ... and Lina learned how a girl could be invisible. Drop your eyes, stare at the ground. Stick to the corners, and the dim side of buildings. Shine too bright, the way Cassie and Misty had, and you would burn out too fast.

The other girls in the Bad Place had two strategies—make themselves larger or make themselves disappear. Those seemed to be the only options for girls in the world outside. If you were normal, weak, people stomped on you. Better to be big or to be too small. The ones who wanted to count puffed themselves up with food and muscle. They stomped through the hallways, slammed doors, asked the others what the hell they were looking at. "Do you have a problem with me? If so, you want to go outside to solve it?"

The other girls got thinner and thinner, mouthing their food and depositing it in napkins to be disposed of later, or purging under the guise of food poisoning. If they weren't brave enough for that they cut themselves in the bathroom, carving out bits of themselves as often as they could. It was common knowledge that you did what you could to survive.

Everyone carried their fears with them. Some girls hoarded food, stuffing candy bars and chips in all the places they thought nobody would look. Others dressed themselves in layer after layer of clothing, as if each sweater would protect them.

They all had their tricks to pass the time. One girl spent hours peeling apart her split ends, staring at her hair with focused precision. Another buried herself in books, carrying one or two with her everywhere, even at dinner, her eyes zipping across the pages faster than anyone could possibly read. They were all broken in different places, and even though the teachers tried to mend them, they weren't stronger at the broken places like everyone said they would be. That was a lie. Lina knew it even then, at sixteen: once broken meant it was easier to shatter the next time.

On the outside, Rainy waited for their mother to die. Lina clung to the pay phone in the dormitory hall, listening for updates. Rainy said that Liza spoke only of the old days, before they were born ... mostly at the oars heading through a Class IV rapid, allowing her raft to kiss the sweet spot on the backside of a rock garden. Trees she had tried to save, trunks wider than she could reach around, trees that were fed by rain and soil and hope.

"She never says your name," Rainy said, a tiny twist of the knife.

The funeral in Boise was brief, the air heavily perfumed and hard to breathe. It wasn't what her mother would have wanted. "Dump my ashes in a river and have a party," Liza had once said, but instead she was buried in a sunbaked cemetery outside of town, no water nearby at all, Rainy choosing what seemed easier in the end.

The Bad Place allowed Lina a two-day leave to attend. Their father didn't even come. He was off somewhere in the Southwest, and sent regrets and flowers, neither of which helped at all.

"What are you going to do now?" Lina asked. Her feet were encased in unfamiliar heels, her coat a somber black that she had borrowed from another girl. The twins had stopped arguing, but the tension remained.

"I have a plan," Rainy said. She lowered her voice. "Danny asked me to marry him and I guess I will."

"But why?" Lina asked. "Do you even love him?" It seemed to her that Rainy treated Danny like an accessory, a purse perhaps, or a scarf.

"I like him fine," Rainy said. "Isn't that more important? From what I've seen, love just complicates things." She indicated the garish flower arrangement their father had sent. "What did it ever do for them? Lina, you have to be practical in this life. So, I'm choosing Danny, even though my heart doesn't have butterflies, or whatever the romance novels tell you you're supposed to feel. He has money from the fire insurance, his parents gave it to him, and so I won't ever be cold, or hungry, or alone. We're moving to Florida."

She turned to face Lina. Her hair swung in a shiny bob, while Lina's hung ragged to her waist. Rainy had carefully lined her eyes with black pencil and filled in her lips with a shocking red color. They did not look alike anymore.

"You've done nothing but mess up your life, Lina. If you

don't watch it, you'll end up like Dad." She lowered her voice as a pair of their mother's friends from the bakery walked by. "Wandering around the world, hurting everyone that loves you."

"I'm not like him," Lina protested, afraid that Rainy was right. "If this is about Cassie and Silas, they made me feel like I belonged. You have to admit that our family was messed up." Rainy nodded, looking away.

"Tell me the truth," Lina continued. "What exactly was your problem with Cassie and Silas?"

"Well, they both were real nutcases," Rainy snapped. "And everybody was talking about you at school. It was embarrassing. They said that you would end up like Cassie. That she stole and slept with married guys for money. That you would do it too. I had to stop them from talking. Don't you get it?"

Lina shivered in the overheated room. She grabbed her sister's arm, nails digging in to the soft fabric of Rainy's black sweater. "What did you do, Rainy? What did you do?"

Rainy wrenched away. "Just what needed to be done. I told the guidance counselor, okay? Ms. Blankenship? I told her that Cassie and Bullet were living up there by themselves in the old shop. Some child protective services lady was poking around in town, asking questions after that."

"How could you do that? That was our secret!"

❖ ❖ ❖

Lina walked back into the Bad Place the next day knowing that something had irrevocably changed between them. Rainy had never forgiven her, both for deserting their mother and for the disgrace Lina had brought on the family. She herself would never forgive Rainy for her betrayal. She and her sister would never live on the same street, never marry brothers, never hang over backyard fences together. Even as the crowd of other broken girls at the Bad Place surrounded her with their clandestine flasks and weekend stories, she had never felt so alone.

In the evenings at the Bad Place the girls curled up on sofas donated by rich people, covering themselves in blankets and lies about how much they wanted to leave. They made up stories about how people waited for them on the outside, how special their lives would be. In the end, nearly every girl cried when graduation came. They hugged each other fiercely and promised to write, but nobody did. They all vanished into the big world without a trace.

Sixteen

I followed Misty's ghost to Hells Canyon," Lina said to Silas.

It had seemed like that, imagining the other girl in her passenger seat unwrapping her usual Snickers bar, both bound for an uncertain future. She realized that she had been following ghosts all her life. First, her father, lost to the mountains, her mother, betrayed by the sun. Cassie, taken by the forest.

A tagalong, Lina had always let someone else lead the way. But now, how could she forge her own path? Cassie would say "get up, brush the dirt off your knees and charge forward."

"It sounds grim," Silas said, and then fell silent. She regarded him as he sat there, thankfully looking at his hands and not at her. Sorrow and anger seemed to fight for space. The joyful, scrappy kid she had known seemed long gone. She was startled out of her assessment by something she could not name, something that didn't fit.

"Someone's here," she whispered, quiet enough for only Silas to hear. "Did you hear that?" A skitter in the pine needles, something that could be mistaken for a small animal seeking shelter. That, or a person trying to walk quietly.

"Just the wind. Lina," Silas said. "What do you think about

hanging here in the valley for a while?" He still wasn't looking at her; she couldn't read his face. "I'm working through how I feel about you, about all of it. But if we can clear the air between us, I'm thinking that I could use a friend. You were my only friend back then and you would be now. Will you stay?"

The sun had dropped below the ridge, leaving behind a faint glow where it had been. Soon all the stars would come out in a sky that no longer seemed familiar. Lina's mind drifted to the animosity she had seen in women's faces and the way nobody in the valley ever forgot one single thing you ever did in your life.

"I would always be the firestarter," she said finally. "No matter what I did or how long I lived here, it would never cancel that out, not ever."

And there was fire season, when thunderheads built up piece by piece, their tops sheer ice, the mating of cloud and ground ... and everyone would remember all over again. She was tired of being known for that one horrific night. Just like she was tired now of being invisible Lina, wizard with car engines, fading into the background unseen. There had to be a way to be big in the world.

"Silas, where do you think the wolves are? Do you think if we howl, they'll answer?"

"They might."

Silas cupped his hands around his mouth. He took a big breath to fill his lungs and started low, his howl echoing through the forest. She could tell it wasn't from a wolf; it sounded less wild, more like a song, but it still could be real and desperate enough to elicit a response.

"Let's do it together," he said.

She copied him, tilting her head back, opening her throat

and letting out a howl. At first, it sounded tentative, unsure. Then she put her body into it, howling as loud as she could, their voices mingling together.

There was no answer, only more rustles in the woods, small creatures stirring as the temperatures dropped. Mice? Rabbits? She wasn't sure.

"Nice try, though," Silas said. "You'll get better."

He studied her, his eyes narrowing.

"You know something," he continued. "You say you're afraid, but I don't think that's it at all. I think it's something else. Something that happened up here, with Cassie. Am I right?"

She sat with her legs pulled in under her arms, the night wind coming up the mountain now in a low, sweet rush. She remembered the matches, falling in a slow arc. It wasn't just fear, she thought. Silas was right about that. It was the enormity of consequence, the way one decision could change a life forever, even something as simple as choosing to wear a silky jacket or a tattered black one without anywhere to grip, should you want to save someone. It was the choice of a swipe of a match. Once you had made such an irrevocable choice, how could you trust any future choices? Better to let life happen to you, as if you were a boulder in a river. Even so, the boulders did not choose to tumble downstream with the force of snowmelt behind them. They were swept away, the same way she had allowed herself to be.

Silas pulled his red flannel sleeping bag over his shoulders. Old school, maybe from the shop days. "All right, Tazlina. Truth. You've got to tell me everything." When she didn't speak, he went on. "You know, I always had in the back of my head that maybe I would walk up here and Cassie would be sitting on the Floor, waiting for me. But I never went, maybe because I knew she wouldn't be. Crazy, right?"

Lina had thought the same thing. She had thought that the postcard had been a clue to a hunt that would end with her finding Cassie. And naturally, it would be up here, where it had all begun and where it had all ended.

"Cassie told me about the lightning," she said, drinking straight from the bottle he handed her. The wine had soured some and went down hard, but she drank again, wanting the warmth and courage it brought her.

"Told you what?"

"The time she was struck by lightning."

He took the bottle from her and drank. "Oh man, I do too much drinking alone. Good to have some company. Now what are you talking about? Cassie wasn't struck by lightning."

"But she said you saved her life. On the Devils staircase one time. She stopped breathing, she actually died, but came back to life. You ran for help. You saved her."

"Oh, Lina." He sighed, handing the bottle back. "I don't know what she told you, but it wasn't true. There was no lightning that struck her. I never saved her life. Think about it. You've been up the Staircase. Remember how far we hiked just to get there? How long it takes to get back down? I ran for help and someone came in time to start her breathing again? How does that make any sort of sense?"

"But she said it. Why would she say it if it wasn't true? The marks on her arm. From the lightning. I saw them. They were there. The lightning flowers."

"Those marks she had on her arm? Those marks were from her. She did it. She took a knife and carved in her arm. I found her doing it one day in the bathroom. She said it made her feel better, that by slicing into her skin she released some of the pain she felt inside. I cried, even though I knew I was too old to cry, and she promised not to do it again. That was why she always wore long sleeves. She knew it made me sad to see it."

She remembered the pattern on Cassie's skin, so like the Trees of Heaven. It seemed impossible that she could have carved such a delicate design herself. Like everything else with Cassie, there would never be a true answer.

"But why? Why would she tell me that if it never happened?"

"My sister," he said, and fell silent for a while. Then, "Is anyone really simple? Because she wasn't, not by a long shot. She had all these layers to her. You'd think you had gotten down to the last one, and there would be something else. I don't know why she lied, Lina. Maybe she wanted you to think she was brave. Maybe she thought if she made up stories that she would be more interesting. She never thought she was quite good enough. Didn't you see that about her?"

Lina hadn't seen that at all. Instead, she had seen what she had wanted to see, a girl who held all the clues on how to move through the world. Cassie had given her hope.

"What else did Cassie lie about?" she asked.

"I keep thinking," Silas said. "Maybe you didn't tell me everything. Maybe you saw her go. Maybe you didn't say anything so that she could escape. Maybe she took a back trail down the mountain, a trail none of us knew about except her. But I know that can't be true. Otherwise, why wouldn't she have come back? She would never have left me. Unless she couldn't find me. Maybe she's still looking."

Lina almost put a hand on his arm and then thought better of it. She could feel how tense he was just by his breath, by how he sat, angled away from her. "I saw her, Silas. I saw what she did."

"But you didn't stick around. You didn't make sure. It could still have happened that way. If anyone could run through flame, Cassie could. What if it's true? What if she is out there somewhere?"

"That's not what happened," she whispered.

"Then tell me what happened. They never found her," Silas said. "They looked."

Lina breathed deep into her bones. She had thought she could skirt around it, that last terrible night, the night when she had followed Cassie and lost her nerve. She should have known that she would have to go back there. It was inevitable, as inevitable as the darkness falling around them. And there was something she had always known: she had never really left. That night had stayed with her for fifteen years. Maybe it was time to finally let it go.

She began.

Seventeen

It was so dark Lina could barely see Silas' profile. He had been quiet a long time.

"I was wearing that stupid jacket," she said. "I gave up a lot of things when I moved here, but I couldn't quite give up that jacket. I don't know why I was even wearing it. It wasn't cold that night. When I got down to the road, the firefighters had to peel it off me. It had started to melt from the heat of the fire. It was trying to melt into my skin."

When he said nothing, she went on. "I had to go after her. We had that fight, and you wouldn't talk to me. I wanted to tell her that I didn't mean it. To tell you that I'd ride with you to school, that I'd sit with you at lunch. But I never got the chance."

"You meant it," Silas said. "Even if you had come back and said you didn't mean it, what do you think would have happened? There was no way we would be friends at school. We both knew what school was like."

He finished off the wine with one long swallow. "Hope you don't mind I drank most of it. We're not fancy, us Van Allens."

He was clinging to that name and the past as much as she was.

Silas had listened to her tell the story, as much as she could tell. Following Cassie up the mountain, the matches, the point

212 · The Lightning Within Us

beyond which she could be saved. He had offered nothing, no reason for why Cassie would have climbed the ghost trail bent on burning the forest. There was still something missing, but Lina could tell she wouldn't learn it. What did it matter anyway? She didn't need to know anything else. Cassie had started a fire for her own reasons, and she would never know them.

Silas lay back on the wooden floor, his head resting on his crossed arms. She could only see his outline, blurred in the growing darkness. If he were fuming with anger or close to tears, she could not tell. His voice gave nothing away.

"I never heard the whole story," he said. "All anyone ever told me was that you came down and Cassie didn't."

Lina slid down as far as she could into her sleeping bag. The first few stars were starting to prick the sky. The trees above her were survivors, somehow resisting the fire Cassie and she had set. In other places the fire had opened the canopy so that light filtered in. In those places grouse whortleberry and heather grew with abandon in great mats. Young trees had come in too, flushed with new growth. Cassie had created a whole new forest.

❖ ❖ ❖

That night Lina dreamed of wolves. Wolves passed through her sleep as fluid as water. It had been a long time since she had dreamed of anything but Cassie.

She allowed herself to believe that it was over, finally.

Silas came back from the spring with water in their bottles. Something had broken loose in him; she could tell by his easy walk and low whistle. Even his voice sounded lighter.

"The mountain doesn't feel empty to me," he said. "It feels like she's here, somehow. Do you feel it too?"

Lina didn't feel anything but the changing forest—trees dying, others reaching for the sun and the sky. The forest had never really been the peaceful place she had imagined. Instead, it was a battleground, a bloodless war in which the armies of plants and animals fought it out. She didn't belong here, neither of them did.

She remembered something. "Cassie said your uncle was getting out of prison. Did you ever hear from him again?"

Silas froze. He stopped stuffing the sleeping bag into his pack. "I don't want to talk about him."

She didn't press him; his face showed an unwillingness to speak.

They sat on the wooden floor together for the last time, neither moving to leave.

"Do you think you'll come up here again?" she asked.

"Maybe," Silas said. "Everything I've read about loss tells me to move on, but I don't know how to do it. There will always be this gap in my heart where she was. I'll always look for her. I guess I'll hike up here now and then, just to see what happens to the place. It can't last forever."

The trees they saw would have to fall someday, weakened by time and wind and snow. The tangled brush that marched in after would hide the wooden foundation, and someday it would cave into the forest floor. Someday there would be no sign it was ever there.

Footsteps in the crunchy pine needles.

"Cassie?" Lina whispered.

But it was a man, a short, stocky man with a camouflage backpack and a gun in his hand ... Tony Ray.

214 · The Lightning Within Us

"Thought I heard voices. Sometimes I think I hear them up here, and then it's only the creek. It can trick you that way up here. Strange echoes, voices when there's nobody within miles. But this time I was right." Tony Ray had been climbing; his breath came in short explosive bursts. *Not in shape. Easy to outrun.*

But the gun. He waved it erratically in their general direction. "You two," he said. "You should have listened to me. I told you not to come up here."

Silas was on his feet and Lina stood up too. Tony Ray was blocking the way out, but did the old trail on the backside of the mountain remain? Could she find it, after all this time? Would he be able to shoot her as she ran?

Tony turned on Lina, the barrel pointing at her chest. He was close enough for her to see sweat beading on his clammy skin. "And you. You always thought you were better than me, you and your twin sister. The two of you, looking down on this valley and the people in it. Everybody knew that about you two, what you were thinking about us. Hicks, rednecks, not worth your precious time."

A blur of movement: Silas, moving toward Tony Ray, who spun back while flicking the gun back and forth in a wild motion.

"Back off," Tony Ray demanded. "I should kill you both. Nobody's going to miss you, Van Allen. Maybe her, maybe not."

"Let's all calm down, please," Silas said. For a moment, Lina saw Bullet again, the kid with the long bangs, who had looked away when his tormentors had called after him, the one who hadn't thrown any punches even when they did.

"You always were a coward," Tony Ray sneered, moving closer to them.

An animal called from far away, and then closer. A howl? She could tell Silas heard it too by the brief glance he allowed before turning back to Tony Ray.

"I have a right to be angry," Tony Ray continued. "Your sister burned my house down and I don't buy that it was an accident."

"But it was," Lina said. "I was there. It was."

Tony Ray laughed, short and without mirth. "I watched you three all that summer," he said, steadying the gun. "I can't believe you never saw me."

Cassie had been right. Someone had been following them.

Fear sizzled down Lina's spine as Tony Ray again swung the gun between the two of them. She forced her eyes open, wanting to scream, waiting for the impact of the bullet.

Tony Ray shifted his backpack from his shoulder to his back. Mistake, Lina thought. The gun was now pointing at the ground.

Lina caught Silas' glance and instantly knew what he was thinking, just like the old days. *Get the gun. One of us distracts him and the other grabs the gun.*

"What's that you're carrying?" Silas asked. "Maybe you should show us."

"None of your business." Turning away to guard the heavy pack from Silas' grasp, Tony Ray lost his balance. In one swift motion, Silas pulled at the backpack, unzipping it, spilling a waterfall of light and color onto the ground. Trying to control the falling contents, Tony Ray dropped the gun. Instinctively, Lina kicked it out of his reach and picked it up, the handle slick with sweat from Tony Ray's hand. She straightened, holding it hidden behind her back. The gun felt too final to use.

Silas let go of the nearly empty bag.

"What the hell?" he said. "You're mining crystals. I knew it."

"So, what if I am? Your kin did it too," Tony snarled.

"People want them bad," Tony Ray said. "Wouldn't you? Just look at them."

Suddenly, he noticed her holding the gun awkwardly behind her. Immediately, he grabbed her arm, twisting it painfully. She elbowed him.

Quickly joining the battle, Silas pulled at Tony Ray's arm, helping Lina lurch from his sweaty grasp. Silas struggled to keep hold, but Tony Ray had a hundred pounds on him and shoved himself free, sending Silas sprawling to the ground with a staggering blow to the face. Tony Ray advanced on Lina. She backed up, both in a desperate dance.

"Give me the gun, Tazlina McCarthy."

There it was, the same fear that she had battled all her life, sweeping over her like a wave. Her breath came in sharp bursts. She pointed the gun at Tony Ray's chest, but he kept coming closer. Silas wasn't moving.

Lina backed up as far as she could, until she was almost at the place where the trail dove down off the mountain, a steep slope behind her.

She caught her breath in a gasp. Behind Tony Ray, Silas was on hands and knees, reaching for the cold chisel that had fallen from the backpack.

Tony took one step, stalking her the way a wolf might, moving slowly and cautiously, calculating the distance between them. Lina wavered, her heart pounding, her fingers slippery on the gun. She felt for the trigger.

"Ask your buddy here what happened to Bert Van Allen," Tony Ray spat. "Ask him about his sister and the rock bar."

Her eyes on Tony Ray, Lina moved, nearly falling backwards. She was trapped. Lina readjusted her grip, her arms shaking from the strength it took to hold the gun upright.

Tony Ray took another step.

"Fire doesn't burn bone," he said. He was close enough that she could see beads of sweat on his forehead.

One more step.

Silas was on his feet now ... moving slowly, heel to toe, the way he had taught her. He was so far away; it would take too long.

"You should have left well enough alone," Tony said. He reached for her arm. It was all over.

Silas came up faster than she would have imagined anyone could move, his fingers wrapped around the cold chisel. But instead of using it, Silas tipped his head back and howled. It was a long, ragged call, not his best, but Lina could hear it echo through the granite and trees and the rivers.

Tony whirled around. "What the hell are you doing?"

Surely, they wouldn't answer. But from somewhere over the next ridge, an answering howl. The others heard it too.

"Go on down the mountain, Tony," Silas said evenly. "You're outnumbered."

There it was again ... a long, ragged plaintive cry, coming closer to where they stood.

Backing away, Tony Ray looked from the gun to the chisel.

"You two are crazy. I'm getting the hell out of here." Turning on his heel, he bolted down the mountain, the sound of breaking branches heralding his passage.

Eighteen

"He's afraid of wolves," Lina said, amazed. "Tony Ray's afraid of wolves."

She couldn't hear his flight anymore; it was as if the mountain had swallowed Tony Ray up. She felt her heart slow, her breathing return to normal. Had that really happened? Nothing in the forest had changed. Light filtering down through the trees the way it had before, touching individual long-needled branches. The smell of a sun-warmed forest. Tiny dusk-colored birds swooping in graceful arcs beneath what was left of the sky. It seemed impossible that everything was still the same.

Silas took a long breath too. "Can't really blame him. He's seen wolves come down in the middle of the night, get in the middle of his cows, only the glow of their eyes. He's seen what they've done to a calf. It's been passed down from his father, and his grandfather before that."

"You feel sorry for him? He said he was going to kill us."

"But he didn't," Silas said. "He might have just wanted to scare us. Guys like Tony, they just puff up like a balloon until someone pricks them."

Another howl, farther away now. Were the wolves following Tony Ray? She hoped so.

"Tony Ray doesn't give up. He bides his time. No doubt he'll hound me, try to drive me out."

"Your uncle," Lina began. She wanted to believe that Tony Ray had lied, but she could imagine Cassie with a rock bar. She had seen her heft one with ease, pounding ferociously on a rock that stood in her way. "Cassie told me what your uncle did to her. Unless that was a lie too."

"I was only five, but I remember knowing something wasn't quite right. I knew he was down on his luck and was living with us. That was when my mother was still around. He was supposed to be looking for a job, to get on his feet, but well, that never seemed to quite happen. Once I was older, I put the pieces together. I remember this one floorboard in her room would squeak if someone walked on it. My room was right next to hers. I woke up almost every night hearing that floorboard. And then the next day I would catch her crying, but she wouldn't say why. It wasn't until years later that she finally told me why Uncle Bert went to prison."

Silas swiped a grimy hand across his face; he was going to have a black eye. Already the skin on his face was swollen and red. It looked painful.

"She always tried to protect me," he continued. "She wanted me to think life was easy ... even though she knew I would find out different."

He sat down hard on the wooden slab. "Ah, hell. Tell me, Lina. What do I do now?"

Silas and Cassie had always been the leaders, Lina the follower. She had climbed single file behind them, placing her feet where they put theirs, trusting that they knew the way. They had known everything she had thought back then. Which mushrooms were safe to collect, what berries would kill her, how to zigzag along a steep slope ... how to survive in a world that was harsh and unforgiving.

"What does your heart tell you to do?"

Silas shrugged. "I don't know what my heart says anymore."

She had to lean forward to hear him.

"I think you should know what really happened," he continued. "The last part of the story. You might as well hear it."

❖ ❖ ❖

Lina thought of a day on the trails, just an ordinary weekday, school still far off in the distance. They had been taking a break in the soft dirt of an underslung trail, and Cassie had started one of her games, the way she often did when she was feeling happy.

"What's your favorite tool?" she had asked, idly pouring dirt through her fingers. "The axe? The loppers?"

Lina had been filthy with dirt that seeped in under her collar and over her boots. "Yeah, what's your favorite tool?" Silas asked. "I mean, if you could only ever use one for the rest of your life. What would it be?"

Cassie loved the rock bar. She loved everything about it, she said. Lina grimaced. "Really?" she asked. "How come?"

"It's not easy to love," Cassie said. "It's hard to carry, and it's heavy. But look at all it can do. You can tamp down dirt around a waterbar, and it'll stay. You can pry out rocks from the trail. And you can smash rocks into little pieces. It's a glorious tool."

Silas loved the chainsaw, because it had a motor. He loved taking it apart and tinkering with it. In the shop, he took the saw and put it in a vice, sharpening the chain with a round file, silver from the shavings glittering on his skin.

Lina had to think about which tool was her favorite. They had a whole arsenal, gathered from wherever Cassie liberated tools. Nobody would miss them, she said, they were rusty and unloved, lying forgotten and cob-webbed in someone's shed or garden. They might as well take them and fix them up, put a new handle on the shovels, file the edge of the pulaski sharp again. Tools were meant to be used, not abandoned in the rain.

"What if someone catches you stealing their tools?" Lina had asked her once, seeing the pile she kept in the shop.

"It's not stealing," Cassie said. "Not really. More like extended borrowing. Anyway, nobody ever catches me. I'm in and out like the wind."

"I like the shovel," Lina had said finally. Silas snickered; the shovel was such a lowly tool. It didn't have the panache of a pulaski or the power of a rock drill. But Lina liked it because it meant something. With a shovel, you could haul away big chunks of dirt that were blocking a waterbar. You could slide it under a recalcitrant rock. In a pinch, you could rig up a pry system and roll a log as wide around as your body off the trail, sending it thundering off into the woods.

"Okay, people," Cassie said. "Grab your favorite tool and get to work." They jumped to their feet and didn't talk about it again.

What else could you do with a rock bar? You could swing it when someone you wanted dead wasn't looking, when they had maybe turned to grab a gun. If you were strong, you could swing it with all the hate and revenge you had stored up inside. It wasn't that different than breaking up a rock, not really. Bones and rock, not all that dissimilar.

❖ ❖ ❖

"She killed him," Lina whispered. "Tony Ray was right. She killed her uncle. And you didn't tell me."

Silas covered his face with his hand. "Believe me, I thought you were going straight home. That's why I told you not to come in. Not because I was angry at you. We had just come down from the Floor, and we had to clean up. It was ... a mess. It was Cassie's idea. She didn't want you mixed up in it. She was trying to protect you."

Lina shivered in her summer coat as he went on, his voice a low monotone. She could picture them, a skinny boy and his sister, bound together with a secret they could not reveal, coming up with a desperate plan.

"We carried the duffel bag up the mountain that afternoon," he said. "Before you came over the second time. Took him up to the Floor. Figured nobody would ever look there. Especially if we let the trail grow over. Pretty soon it would look like nobody had been up there in a hundred years."

Lina moved a few steps away until her back collided with a tree. Under the soft cloth of her coat, she imagined she could feel the tree's heartbeat, water and sugar and sunshine moving through the bark and the trunk and the leaves. The tree felt good, solid, even though she knew that its roots were likely weakened by the long-ago fire. It could, she knew, fall without warning.

Silas was still talking, his words unspooling into the clearing. "We dug a grave near the Floor, down in the jackpots where all the fallen trees were. Used the pulaski and shovel. Hauled some rocks to lay on top, to keep out the critters."

"But the fire. Why did Cassie start the fire?"

"You know something, Lina? I always thought it was you that started the fire. Not Cassie. You. I thought you started the fire that killed her. Now you're telling me it wasn't your idea. That it was hers."

"Me? Why would it have been me?"

"Well, you know there was something between you and Cassie. I could feel it. Love and envy. You were jealous of her. Weren't you?"

"I loved her," Lina whispered.

"I loved her," she repeated, her voice stronger. "I would never have hurt her."

"I guess I believe you," Silas said, but his voice sounded as if he really wasn't sure at all. "My sister, she was different that summer. She always thought someone was following her."

He paused, swallowing hard.

"That night was terrible. We got back from the Floor and cleaned everything up, and then we just sat there. Not saying anything. I think we both knew nothing would ever be the same. And then she headed out the door. I asked where she was going, but who knew with her. I thought maybe she was just going to lift a couple of tools."

"I saw you," Silas said. "With the gun pointed at Tony Ray. You were ready to kill him. I saw it in your eyes."

Lina realized she was still holding the gun. She unwrapped her fingers from it, the blood coming back into her hands, and dropped it to the ground. "I didn't, though," she said. "I stopped."

He shrugged as though he didn't believe her. "Well. Anyway. All I can ask is not to tell. To forget what you heard here."

What good would it do now? Choices with unintended consequences. Trees of Heaven, evil or good ... or a little bit of both.

"I'm looking forward to the snow closing the road," Silas

said. "To the west, over Himes Summit, they sometimes leave it closed on account of avalanches. If we're lucky, Evergreen closes too. They always get that one open eventually, but until they do, it's like we're locked in here, hidden away. Nobody can get in and nobody can get out. I like it that way."

You could leave, Lina started to say. He could go anywhere, throw a pin at a map. But how could he truly start over with so much to carry. Sadness, regret, loss—an invisible backpack he could never shed.

He hesitated, turning from the scarred landscape to briefly make an uneasy eye contact.

"We aren't going to see each other again, are we?"

She shook her head. A breeze carrying the promise of an early winter moved through the trees. Soon, like he had said, the snow would begin to fall. It would cover all the empty places among the trees, the broken pockets that had once held translucent crystals, the secrets that still hid there.

She didn't want to see Cassie anymore. She didn't want the wind to keep her awake, tallying up all her fears. It was time to let Cassie go. To do that, she had to let Silas go too.

"All right then. It's done," Silas said. He reached out for her hand and she walked over to him. Like Cassie's so long ago, his hand radiated heat. "So long, Tazlina."

"Aren't you coming?"

"I'm going to stay up here awhile," he said. "You go on. You know the way."

It was hard to let go of his hand.

"You know, I could never picture Cassie old," he said. "Could you?"

"No," she answered. "Always seventeen."

"Young ... untamed ... beautiful." Silas tried to smile but couldn't.

Lina remembered the postcard, the reason she had come back to the valley. Pulling it out of her coat pocket, she handed it to Silas.

"What is it?" he asked. He glanced at the picture on the front and flipped it over. "Lina. Where did you get this?"

"Left on my father's car," she said. "He brought it to me. You haven't seen this before?"

"What? No. Is this some kind of a joke?"

"Is it from her?" Lina breathed. "Is that her handwriting?"

He stood, staring down at the card. "I don't know. She didn't write much. It could be. It looks familiar. Yes, it might be. But is it possible?"

Silas sat back down again and put his head in his hands.

"Unbelievable," he said in a muffled voice. "I need to find her."

There was nothing else to say.

❖ ❖ ❖

Silas was right. Her body knew the way to go, down the tight switchbacks where they had hauled rocks to hold the unstable soil, through the narrow tunnel of thorny brush, past the rock wall, past the ghost trees the fire had left behind. She came out of the mountains with her coat torn, buttons missing off her shirt, the mountain attempting to take everything it could from her.

❖ ❖ ❖

She had so many choices, both terrifying and exhilarating. She could drive back across the border, up the Kleinschmidt grade, and down into the Imnaha canyon. She could go back up to her cabin on Starvation Road, to work at the auto shop. She could stay there at the end of the road. Or she could spread out an atlas, look across the map, and drive on into a new life.

She thought about the settlers of Hells Canyon and their fateful decision to bring in shade. Every action had consequences. Everyone made choices, sometimes right and sometimes wrong.

Cassie and the fire. Lina would never know the reason; only that it would take one match to land in a bed of kiln-dry pine needles that had been stored up since June. A light wind had taken charge then, pushing the fire into a stand of overgrown trees, their branches acting like ladders to the sky. Emboldened, the fire climbed higher, chewing up the forest. It was too late to stop it, even if Cassie had wanted to.

"There's only five reasons why anyone does anything," Cassie used to say. If Lina tried hard enough, she could still see Cassie—her mass of untamed hair, her sharp chin, her eyes as blue as one of the crystals Tony Ray had stolen—sitting cross-legged in the trail, counting the reasons off on her fingers. Love, sex, revenge, money and anger. "We clear the ghost trails for love," she had said. "I do everything else for revenge."

"Against what?" Lina asked then. She could see herself too, a wide-eyed young girl, unbaked as bread dough, scabs on her knees from falling on rocks, messy hair caught up in a bandanna. Lina felt sorry for the girl she had been, so caught up in worrying about what others thought, waiting for someone to tell her the right path.

"Do you even know how the world works, Tag?" Cassie had asked. "You're lucky if you can't even imagine revenge. Do everything for love for as long as you can."

❖ ❖ ❖

As she opened the door to her Bronco, Lina turned and looked back at the mountains. There was a moment when she thought she could stay here in the valley. She would clean up the house her parents had bought, toss out all the packrats, plant flowers. She could grow old here, watching the forest grow old too. In another fifty years, when she was eighty, all the people who remembered the fire would be gone. Besides, even without the help of humans, fires happened about every hundred years. It was a way that the forest started over from scratch. An entirely new forest came to take its place. Maybe in another few decades, the forest would replace itself again.

But she knew she couldn't stay. This was not home, never truly had been. Perhaps home was down on a dry desert playa with a man who could teach her how to open her heart, to lean against someone instead of leaning on them. Or maybe once she passed the turnoff to Fields Station, down there in the Great Basin where the high desert hoarded all the water, she would keep on driving to somewhere else. She wasn't sure, but she knew she needed to find out. Cassie had always told her to go with her heart. The heart, she said, was the most important thing. It was what kept everything stable, whether it be a rock wall or a person. Her heart told her to go.

She climbed into her car and turned the key. Running rough, she thought. Nothing that some new spark plugs and premium oil couldn't fix. She placed her foot on the gas and drove down the road without looking back. She didn't want to know if Silas had followed her quietly down the trail, stood there watching her blink out of sight, waiting for her to merge with all the other cars carrying people out of the valley to uncertain futures. She didn't want to see his face as he turned the postcard over and over in his hands. She didn't want to change her mind.

She remembered again the Trees of Heaven, and the shade-starved settlers who had brought them in. Had they not known that the trees would destroy the native vegetation and establish a stronghold in the canyon, resisting all efforts to eradicate them? Had the settlers decided that whatever happened down the line didn't matter as much as precious, life-sustaining shade now?

The Trees of Heaven and Cassie, both beautiful and evil at the same time.

As Lina drove out of the valley, she was sure she would never see again, she decided that probably the Hells Canyon settlers were only told that these new trees grew fast and stubborn, a good match for a place where most things had to fight to survive.

But even if they knew the truth, the settlers had chosen shade.

Nineteen

It had been nearly a year since Lina had seen Silas. She had traveled west to the Pacific Ocean, started taking classes to counsel troubled teenagers. It was a different life, but one she was growing to like.

Arriving home on a near perfect afternoon, Lina found a letter in the mailbox, postmarked from a place she had finally put behind her. The handwriting was spiky, as if pressed hard against the paper.

Silas?

Dear Lina,

I have news. The Forest Service has opened up the old trails, some of them following the paths the three of us created, past the rock walls we built, over the waterbars.

And there's this. A few hikers have seen glimpses of a woman, who fades away into the trees when she sees them. They say she seems to be badly burned, but strong.

I don't know, Lina, but I've got to find her. I won't stop looking.

Silas

Lina walked to her window. A hundred feet below, the ocean worked the shore, the tide coming in. She knew the wilderness could make you see or hear things that aren't there. A stump that looks like a bear. The sound of a voice instead of a river.

Still, she wanted to believe Cassie was alive. She could see it clearly—herself, running half-blind down the trail, and Cassie, because she knows the mountain so well, taking the uncleared path down the other side of the mountain.

Of course, in the clear light of morning, Lina knew this was impossible, that she saw Cassie dive into the flame.

Lina stared at the ocean, the incoming tide covering up all the footprints in the sand, water endlessly polishing every rock.

"Maybe," she mumbled to herself.

She closed her eyes, picturing her father roaming across the Great Divide, hunting treasure. Joe, somewhere in the Great Basin, yearning for someone to make him feel whole. Silas, high on a mountain, searching for a ghost.

And herself, living here above the restless sea, trying to rewrite her past by helping girls like her stay out of bad places. All of them with their own Trees of Heaven, their own lightning caged deep inside.

❖ ❖ ❖

Once upon a time a girl dove into flame. There was a moment when her body hung suspended between sky and earth, a moment when she could have taken it back, the same moment when Lina could have saved her. Instead, like most moments people remember and regret, she did nothing.

Lina remembered that Cassie flew, the way she always had wanted to do. Lina couldn't imagine that Cassie would ever come down, she was that high. Lina remembered that Cassie was smiling. She remembered that the sight of Cassie flying took her breath away.

About the Author

Mary Emerick

A former wilderness ranger, widland firefighter and trail crew member, Mary Emerick lives in Oregon where she loves to hike, ski and chase after Siberian huskies.

The author of three other titles which feature the relationship between people and nature, changing climates, and wild landscapes, she has also written for anthologies and environmental journals.

Her goal is to inform, educate, and inspire people to appreciate and care for wild places.

Visit her website at: *maryemerick.com*.

Other Books by Mary Emerick

The Geography of Water (University of Alaska Press)

Fire in the Heart: A memoir of friendship, loss, and wildfire (Arcade)

The Last Layer of the Ocean: Kayaking through love and loss on Alaska's wild coast (Oregon State University Press)

Acknowledgments

Thank you to the staff of Hidden Shelf Publishing House, especially Bob Gaines, who skillfully managed to help create what was a meandering path into the novel you are reading.

If you enjoy walking on trails, please consider donating your time or funds to the agency or volunteer group that maintains them to ensure that people who come after us are still able to spend time there.

Explore the Hidden Shelf

Made in the USA
Middletown, DE
15 July 2024

57337934R00136